Byron

THE GRANT BROTHERS SERIES BOOK 4

KATHI S. BARTON

WCP
World Castle Publishing
Pensacola, Florida

Copyright © Kathi S. Barton 2011
ISBN: 9781937593476

First Edition World Castle Publishing October 1, 2011
http://www.worldcastlepublishing.com

Cover: Karen Fuller
Editor: Brieanna Robertson

Chapter One

Taylor Bennett was sitting on the bench in the Quad when Jamie Grant came up and sat down beside her. She didn't need to look to see that it was him; she just knew. He had a way about him that she loved and recognized that she didn't have with others, years of friendship.

"Well, are you going to tell me what you've decided or are you going to make me stew some more? You know that I'll keep asking you, daily if need be." Jamie had asked her this same question three times over the past four days. She knew she couldn't put it off any longer.

"I'm never having sex with you," she told him as she leaned forward to pick up her backpack. Everything she had with the exception of clothes was in this thing.

"God, no!" Glancing at him sharply, she thought she could and should be offended, but she knew what he meant.

They had met six years ago at a frat party. Taylor had been there with another girl and they were being harassed by one of the oversized frat boys. When Jamie had come to her rescue, she ended up needing to save his butt from being beaten to a pulp. After the party, she had taken him to his house to clean up his bloody nose and they had started to make out. After the second kiss, both decided it was just too creepy and had become friends instead. Besides, he had the most charming smile.

"It's only temporary. I have to get back on my feet. I can't depend on you to save me all the time. Deal?" She wanted to cry, but that would solve nothing.

"Yeah. On your feet then I kick your butt out. Deal. And the dinner thing this weekend, you'll still be my date? I'll still pay for half the dress, even though I don't mind paying for the whole thing." She had hoped he would forget that as part of the bargain, but nodded at him.

"Yeah, I'll go. But we had a deal. Half and not a cent more. If I didn't need the money, I'd say I'd do it, but..."

"Yeah, your boss sucks and you work for a cheap son-of-a-bitch. I'll see you at the house later."

He kissed her quickly and took off running across the Quad to his office. Taylor picked up her purse and slung her pack over her shoulder and went to the office just off Broad, the crappy office she worked in. Tears pulled at her eyes, but she refused to let them fall.

Two weeks ago, she had a crappy apartment that she shared with two other girls. Her name had been on the lease the first year and then the landlord had never said anything about a renewal so the girls continued to live there. Taylor paid her rent to him directly every month and paid her portion of the bills — cable/Internet and the water bill. She never ate there so didn't contribute to the food, preferring to put her water in her room and drink it warm.

Then one afternoon, she came home from work and Mr. Sharp met her at the door. She smiled at him and he grimaced back. He handed her the mail and asked her to come into his office.

"I'm evicting the three of you the day after tomorrow. I'm sorry, Taylor, but I can't keep hoping they'll pay their rent. They're nearly six months behind and the electric company called today and told me that it's not been paid either."

"Six months! How...I mean, they said everything was fine. I asked and asked." Cherry's parents were supposed to pay the rent while she was in school, Debra had a job as a bartender, and she took care of her third. Six months meant that they owed three thousand in rent — back rent, Taylor corrected.

"I can pay it. It'll wipe me out, but I'll pay it." It wouldn't only wipe her out, but it would take her food money too. But she needed a place to live.

"I'm sorry, honey. I knew that you'd say that and I can't let you do that. They'll never pay you back and they will only do it again if they know that you'll bail them out. The reason I'm telling you now is so that you can get your things out now. When the police come, they will lock everything up until I get my money from those two. You aren't named so you won't have to pay. I have my sons here and they'll help you carry your things out tonight. In two days, the cops are going to put a lock on the door and then sell off their stuff to try and get my money."

She left him after making arrangements to have Peter and Daniel Sharp come up after the girls left for the night and went to her apartment to start packing up. Two hours later, Taylor had put all her belongings in one large trash bag and was sitting on the bed when the Sharps knocked.

Her clothes were all she really had and not a lot of those. Her computer was the only thing of real value that she had and she took it with her everywhere. In a fit of what she could only think of as pure stupidity, she called her best friend and sobbed the entire thing to him. He came to get her at the Scarlet and Gray, a bar on campus, and took her home with him. After a night of ice cream, pizza, and too much beer, he had asked her to move in with him. She refused and had been living in her car until five days ago.

It was raining harder than she had ever seen it since moving to Ohio. The lightning was streaking across the sky like someone had pissed off an electrician and he was waving a live wire over her car. But it was the man that broke her window to get to her that terrified her more. He had pulled her out of the car window through all the broken glass by her hair and tried to rape her. Had the campus police not come by when they did, she was sure he also meant to kill her. As it was, she had twelve stitches in her arm and a bruised face. Jamie had had a fit when he saw her when he had picked her up at the hospital and took her home with him. Again. She had been there since.

Taylor sat at her little desk that morning and set up her things to work. The stupid owners wouldn't replace her computer when the one they provided her broke three months ago, so she had been using hers since. She hated her job with a passion, but needed the income more than she needed to quit. Especially now that she had to save her money to get another place of her own.

7

She was an accountant/secretary/receptionist/idiot—high on the idiot part for—Freedom Fighters. The law firm she worked for was an ambulance chasing sort. The pay was crappy, there were no benefits, and she didn't trust that each week her check wouldn't bounce. It had five times now in the five years she had worked for them and she had gotten into the habit of cashing it now before depositing the money into her account. Jason Freedom, one of the two Freedoms she worked for, got pissy with her every week when he realized what she was doing. She just continued doing it. She couldn't afford another seven hundred dollars in bounced check fees again.

She had already decided not to have roommates this time. She thought it might be nice to have her own place with her own things surrounding her. But then snorted to herself and thought what things did she think she was going to put around? Her hairbrush or maybe the collection of under things she secretly bought.

And that was another thing. If she didn't spend eighty-five dollars on a bra and panty set, she might be able to afford her own place sooner. But when she shifted in her hard seat and felt the decadent silk rub against her body, she thought it was well worth the wait.

At five-thirty, she gathered up her things, shut down her computer, and left the office. She had seen neither lawyer today, which suited her just fine, and headed to her new home. Jamie wouldn't be in for another hour, so she decided to fix dinner for them. Trying to decide which pizza place to order from, her only ability in the cooking department, she was startled when the phone rang as she reached for it.

"Hello, Grant residence." She didn't say Grant/Bennett residence; she was only there temporarily. Besides, she hadn't discussed that part of the arrangement with Jamie yet.

"I need to talk to Jamie; put him on the phone." The voice barked at her. She looked at the caller ID and realized it was one of his brothers—Byron, the artist.

She had never met the Grants, any of them. In the years she had known Jamie, it had never come up. They were not dating, and they had no other ties other than being friends, so as far as she knew, they had no idea she even existed. She knew who they were because Jamie talked about them all the time, but that was it.

"Sorry, he's not home from work yet. Can I take a message? I'll make sure he gets it as soon as he gets in." Taylor picked up a pen and was ready. He didn't say anything for several seconds and she looked to see if he had hung up. Nope, still there.

"If Jamie isn't home, then what, pray tell, are you doing there? Robbing the place? I'll have you know that one of his brothers is a lawyer and he'll sue your ass for everything you have if you even try that trick." She knew that she had a temper. She had learned to control it, but it had been a really shitty day—no, week—and she snapped.

"Yes, I'm robbing the place, asshole. It's a new thing in would-be robbers; we answer the phone of our victims and offer to take messages before we ransack the house for valuables. It's a new service we offer and since I have you on the phone, maybe you can give me your opinion of how you think we might improve our service. We are always looking for pricks such as yourself to give us feedback." She took a deep breath before she continued. "Jamie isn't here. You want to talk to him, then fucking call back." The phone slamming into the receiver made her feel somewhat better, especially since she could hear him talking as she had done it. Leaving Jamie a note, she put her coat on and went out into the evening cold.

It was snowing again, she realized with a start. Ohio had the stupidest weather. One day it could be fifty degrees, and the next one, five below. The ground wasn't all that cold yet, but she was sure it would be for this weekend and snow would be perfect for the charity ball she had agreed to go to with Jamie on Friday.

Realizing she still needed a dress, she headed for the second hand shop on campus. He had told her it was very fancy so she had some idea what she needed, but didn't have a great deal to spend. Jamie had offered to pay half for her dress, and if it came to that, she would take him up on the offer.

She found two that she really liked and tried on the first one. After that, there was no reason to try on the other. It fit perfectly and it was in her price range. She stood before the three sided mirror and looked at her reflection.

The dress was a dark blue sheath that hugged her slim body tightly until it reached her knees, then flared out to twice the width. The top, or what there was of it, started at the top of her breasts and molded against her. The built in bustier, which lifted her breasts, held the dress up firmly and showed off her ample cleavage very nicely. Turning slightly, she noticed that the back dipped dangerously low and showed the dimples of her ass when she moved. Frowning, she wondered if someone as tall as Jamie could see down the dress and get a view of her rump. Still trying to get a good look, the owner of the little shop came up to stand behind her.

"The dress was made for you, honey. Damn, but I don't think I've ever seen anyone fill it out quite the way you have."

"Yeah, I have big boobs. Do you think my date will be able to get a nice peak of my ass crack when we dance? I mean, it looks really pretty and all, but I'm not into this guy that way and I'd just as soon keep my more prominent parts to myself."

The proprietor, Alice, threw back her head and laughed. Then she walked up to stand in front of Taylor, stood up on her tippy toe, and bent slightly to look. Catching Taylor's gaze in the mirror, she winked.

"First of all, nope, no butt crack. Secondly, no one is going to notice your butt when they have a much nicer view from your front. Any man that dances with you is going to be hard pressed, if he isn't already pressed hard, to see anything but the way the dress matches your eyes perfectly. Or that the light bouncing off your hair arches like dark moon beams. You look very beautiful, my dear. Where are you going, if you don't mind my asking?"

"The annual charity thing his mother puts on at the Polaris Center. I guess it's really fun. Have you ever been there?" When she didn't answer, Taylor turned to look at her.

"You know the Grants? No, I've never...you came to my shop to get a dress for the biggest event of the season? I'm so...wow! No, I've never had that sort of money to go. I heard it's like a thousand bucks a plate to go and the auction generates nearly a million dollars for whatever charity the mistress deems worthy. I think its child abuse again this year. Last year they raised nearly seven hundred fifty thousand to build a home for children to be safe. And you're going. You're very lucky."

Taylor didn't think she was. So she just smiled at the woman and went to the changing room to take the dress off.

In the few years she had been friends with Jamie, she had managed to avoid his family completely. She knew all about them. Jamie was very close to them and he talked about them all the time. And he had on more than one occasion invited her to their outings and just for dinner, but she had never gone. And now, she thought, I'm trapped. Without a place to live and not a lot of money, she had agreed to go because he had asked her to after he had generously offered her a place to stay. Hanging up the dress, she stepped into the shop again.

"I'll take it. And do you have a wrap that will go with it? It's getting cold and I don't think my coat will look very good with this."

Even with the purchase of the dress and wrap and then a bus ride to the mall for shoes, she was still under budget. Smiling and pretty proud of herself, Taylor decided to stop by the new club in the area that she had heard of.

Taylor opened the door to Jamie's house several hours later than she had wanted. She knew that she would never go back to that club. She hurt everywhere. Without stopping to look around, she went to her bedroom to take a much needed bath before bed.

Chapter Two

Byron saw a flash of someone running past the living room and then nothing. He had been waiting for the smart-assed woman to come back for almost three hours and he wasn't getting any happier with each passing minute. He wanted to give her a piece of his mind, first for being smart, then for hanging up on him. He had already talked to Jamie, catching him at the University, and he had told him he wouldn't be home until later.

When Byron had asked Jamie about the woman who answered the phone, Byron had nearly gone through the roof when he found out that she was now living with his brother.

"What are you going to tell Mom, huh? You just going to say 'hey, Mom, meet the new squeeze?' I'm sure that'll go over great! She's going to castrate you. You know that, don't you?"

"You know, you really should mind your own business. I'm an adult and who I have staying in my own home is none of your fucking business. Let me handle Mom."

"Handle Mom? Are you insane? She'll handle you, young man." Byron was only sixteen months older than Jamie, but he sometimes felt like he was decades.

Jamie hung up on him and Byron had gotten into his car and drove to Jamie's house to have it out with the woman and throw her out if he didn't like what he was seeing. That had been two hours and fifty-three minutes ago. He stalked up the stairs and was just about ready to just start yelling her name at the top of his lungs when he heard the music coming from one of the bedrooms down the long hallway.

Walking through the bedroom, he glanced at the dress bag on the bed and a backpack on the chair and little else. Steam billowed out from the bathroom door as he turned the knob, and he was surprised to feel it turn easily. Stupid woman, he thought, she didn't even lock the door. She was probably hoping for Jamie to come home and join her in the tub and trap him. Before he could push it open, the door was jerked from his hand and opened.

He didn't know who was more shocked, her or him. She stood there with her dark hair down and a towel draped around her front, staring at him. He really couldn't see her face well with the lighting from the bathroom behind her and no lights in the bedroom on, but he could see enough to know she wasn't anything like he had thought. Before him stood the bane of his horrible day. But he had to hand it to her; she didn't scream or go into hysterics like he thought she would when confronted by a stranger.

"What the fuck are you doing in my room? And where is Jamie? Get out!" She took a step toward him when he glanced in the mirror behind her.

"Christ! Who did that to you?" She turned to see what he meant, saw her own reflection, and turned back to look at him. His breath caught.

She was beautiful. Her hair wasn't just dark, but almost a blue-black. Eyes the deepest blue that made him think of the Caribbean ocean. She wasn't overly tall, but stood around five foot nine inches in her bare feet. Skin the color of fresh baked biscuits his mother's cook made for Sunday dinners looked soft and warm, touchable and fresh. The way the towel draped over her breasts, he imagined them to be full and heavy, and he found himself suddenly wondering if her nipples were large as well. He started toward her when she suddenly backed up again and slammed the door in his face. He heard the lock click.

"Now you lock the door? I'm not leaving until you...come out of there right now. I want to have a look at your back." Byron suddenly knew what had happened to her.

There were perhaps twenty welts across her back that he could see clearly, red and angry-looking. He was sure had he been able to look at her chest there would have been similar marks there as well. He knew there would be a red place at both of her ankles and

14

around each wrist and probably around her throat. He knew without a doubt that Ms. Taylor Bennett had been tied to a St. Andrews Cross and beaten probably as recently as today.

"I know you're Jamie's brother, but I don't know which one. I don't give a rat's ass either. I want you to leave right now. He said that I would have privacy and this is an invasion of it. Go away, now," she said to him through the door.

"I don't think so. I said to come out so that I can have a look at those marks. Some of them are too raw, which means that whoever you're playing with got too rough. Christ, did Jamie do that to you? Damn it, come out right now!"

"No! I said to go the fuck away. Are you deaf? I'm going to call the police." He looked at the bed when the house phone went off. Smiling, he knew he was safe from that threat.

"Byron? What the...what are you yelling about? Taylor? Are you...what's going on here?" Byron leaned his head against the bathroom door. Jamie would pick now to come home. He chuckled when he heard the woman on the other side of the door begin to cuss like a sailor.

"I was just asking your...girlfriend?"

The door flew open so quickly, he nearly fell on top of her. As it was, he had to grab her to steady himself. Her hiss had him jumping back away from her quickly.

"Jamie, could you please take this...this uncivilized barbarian downstairs? I want to go to bed."

"Uncivilized bar...oh no, you don't. I asked you a question. Who did..." He stopped when she shook her head at him. It was a small shake, but enough to tell him that Jamie hadn't hurt her, but that he also knew nothing about the marks. There was also the terror in her eyes.

Jamie must have sensed her distress, because he came over and hugged her to him. When Taylor moaned and paled, Byron wanted to tell him to let her go, but with a short kiss, Jamie stepped away from her. Taylor grabbed the door jamb for support but said nothing. No one said anything for several moments then Jamie moved toward the door and said good night to Taylor. Byron had no choice but to follow.

15

After getting two beers, Jamie joined Byron in the living room. When he started in on his new office and promotion, Byron only listened with half an ear. He couldn't wrap his mind around Jamie's girlfriend. She liked to play. When there was a lull in the conversation, Byron decided to get some information.

"What's the relationship between you and Ms. Bennett? I mean, you said she lived here. What are your living arrangements?" Byron asked him.

"She is living here until she gets back up on her feet. She's had some financial difficulties lately and I'm just helping her out. Stay out of it, Byr. Taylor would do the same for me." That told him nothing, but when Jamie yawned for the third time in as many minutes, Byron left.

He was suddenly sure they were not sleeping together. She would be hard pressed to explain the marks if he was seeing her naked. And Byron was reasonably sure that his little brother didn't swing that way. Smiling to himself, he was also reasonably sure that no one would peg him for a player either.

Byron had never told anyone, especially not his family, that he was a Dom. And not only was he a Dom, but he was a very good one. Early in his sexual experimentations, he had discovered that he enjoyed dominating his sexual partner and over the years had developed a taste for all sorts of different ways to make someone yield. He enjoyed what he liked to call vanilla sex, and his partners never knew that he was anything but a considerate and consummate lover. Only once in all his years had he ever tried anything with someone outside of the clubs he went to and that had turned out badly.

Her name had been Dawn Miller. She had worked for him for a few months as a clay assistant and they had gotten along well. After a few dates, he had gone back to her place and they had spent the entire night making love and talking. When she brought up that she wanted to be tied to the bed and spanked, he said he would do it.

He was new to the world of Dom/Sub and had made several mistakes that night. Mostly it wasn't noticing that she was very experienced. Also, and most importantly, how eager she had been to be flogged. Byron had whipped her several times, leaving marks all over her back and her lovely ass. Two mornings later, he was being asked to come downtown to answer a few questions about abuse to the woman. He was lucky in that his brother's friends had come to get him and that they didn't think he'd done anything to the girl. Dawn was claiming that he had beaten and raped her.

He had no more gotten to the jail when she called him on his cell phone to tell him what she had done. Byron, thinking fast, had put the phone on speaker and let the cops listen in on what she said.

She told him how she had done this sort of thing before and that if he paid up now, she would leave him alone and drop the charges. He played along with the encouragement of the officers and told her he would give her anything she wanted. She demanded thirty thousand dollars for now, and more later, and told him where to meet her. He did his part and she went off to jail for blackmail. After that, he was more careful.

~~~

Taylor was sitting at her desk the next morning when Jamie called to tell her he was leaving for his mom's.

"Are you sure you can't get off work and come with me? I can't believe you have to work tomorrow. Doesn't your boss have any kind of heart?"

"I doubt it, but no, I can't get off. They seem to think there will be a mad rush of deep fried turkey lawsuits and they don't want to miss a one. You have fun. You know I don't care for this sort of thing anyway. Call me tonight and give me the scoop on the big announcement."

His brother, Spencer, who got married in July, said he had an announcement to make. Jamie was pretty sure it was that his wife was pregnant and he was excited about the prospect of being an uncle again. Taylor was just glad not to be a part of the whole thing. She was also glad to be away from his brother, Byron. Taylor was pretty sure he wasn't going to let go what he had seen in the mirror. She shifted in her chair and thought about what he hadn't seen in her reflection.

The Dom at the club had hurt her — badly. And no matter how many times she had said her safe word, he wouldn't stop. The wound on her thigh was the most painful. He had bitten her hard

17

enough to leave deep teeth marks in several other places as well as the one on her thigh. Thankfully, he hadn't drawn blood. Then there were the lacerations on her belly too. And the wounds on the backs of her thighs made it extremely difficult to sit for very long. Two of them, made from the leather whip he had produced from a closest and not on her approved list of things he could use, were deep enough that she feared she might need stitches.

It never entered her mind to go to the police. She knew what they would say, that she had given him permission to do those things to her simply by being the sort of deviant that she was. She felt tears threaten to spill and wiped at them furiously. She had to work, not mull over something she couldn't change. After hanging up with Jamie making arrangements for him to pick her up on Friday night, she started inputting the clients' payments into their files.

She was perhaps an hour into it when she realized she had written the same number more than once. Frowning, she scrolled the ledger back up and found the number. After checking the account, she was surprised to find it was the same exact number. Then she noticed it twice more. Hitting control F, she put in the number, including the cents, and had it search—nine hundred thirty-three dollars and twelve cents. It found twenty-six entries with the same number. Curious, she took off the change and had it do another search for just the dollar amount and when the number popped up, she sat back in her chair hard, causing injury to her thigh. Three hundred and fifty times, and the change difference was only a few pennies off with each different entry.

Taking out one of her steno pads, Taylor began writing down the account number and the amount each deposit was. She was just thinking about how much was being deposited in this account when she came across a name she knew. Mary Jane Stone—she had made six deposits into the account since May. Six deposits made as a dead woman. Randomly, Taylor picked another name and did an Internet search for them. Roger Steward died two years ago and hadn't missed a single payment. She did this for three more names and came up with the same results, their deaths long ago or as recent as eighteen months.

Going to the huge file cabinet armed with the account numbers, Taylor took the five names she had discovered and pulled their files. She wasn't a lawyer and she knew nothing about the files and what she was reading, but she knew how to run a copier. Taking the files over to the little machine, she made copies of every piece of information in the file, including the death notices, and put them into her backpack.

Sitting back at her desk, all she could think about was that movie, The Firm and the scam that those lawyers had been running. And Wilford Brimley and that white-haired guy chasing Tom Cruise all over the place trying to kill him. She was afraid, terrified really, knowing that whatever she had discovered wasn't only illegal, but with the amount of money they were collecting off the dead, it could get her dead. Of the three hundred and fifty times she had found it for just this year, an amount of over three hundred and twenty-five thousand dollars, she wondered how many others there were for different amounts.

At five o'clock, she locked everything down and started to pack up her computer. Biting her lip, she opened the file and pulled out her thumb drive. She made a copy of everything on her computer that was the firm's and put the full drive in her sock. On the way home, she was picking up another drive and opening a safety deposit box at the bank too. From now on, she was making copies of everything.

Thanksgiving morning found Taylor at work at eight. She hadn't slept well the night before, pain and embarrassment being high on her list of stress. Then there was the added knowledge that she had those files in Jamie's house. She was terrified that at any minute someone was going to break down the door, storm into her room, and demand what the hell she was doing with company files. After tossing and turning for hours, she decided that she was going to put everything back, shred the copies she had made, and keep her mouth shut.

At nine-thirty, there was a knock at the office doors and a delivery man stood there in the blustering cold. The snow had started at around three in the morning and it was now covering everything in a thick coat of white fluff.

"I'm sorry," she told Tim from 'Rachel's Roses.' "There isn't anyone here today, just me. Could you maybe take them to the owner's house for me?" Jason and Paul Freedom often got flowers and other things delivered to the office, mostly from the flock of women that they hung out with.

"Sure, but aren't you Taylor Bennett? These are for you, honey. If you want, I could take them to your house, but I think the guy who sent them wanted you to enjoy them today."

She squealed. Never in all her life had anyone sent her flowers before. Excited beyond reason, she grabbed Tim's arm and practically threw him into the entrance hall. The long, white box was heavy when she took it from him after signing for it. And after kissing him on the weathered cheek, she skipped to her desk and opened the box.

White tissue paper covered the contents and the card on the top had her name on it in a very bold script that she recognized immediately. Opening it with shaky hands, she read what Jamie had to say.

To my best friend on this day of Thanksgiving. Have a lovely holiday and I promise to bring you back some mashed potatoes.

Love, Jamie

Crying openly now, she opened the paper and burst into tears. He was perhaps the sweetest man she knew and he would remember that she loved mashed potatoes above everything else. There nestled in the paper wasn't long stem roses, because he knew that she was allergic, not carnations, not even daisies, but a large turkey and dressing frozen dinner, a box of her favorite tea bags, and a plate with silverware. There was a long, tapered candle and even a holder for it. Also, deep within, there was a mug and a lighter — and another note.

We'll be eating at six, sit down with your fake dinner and join me at that time. I'll be thinking of you.

Love you, Jamie

The rest of her day went by quickly. She kept thinking about the dinner now in the mini fridge that she had purchased second hand when she had gotten her first and only raise six months after working for the Fighters. The phone never rang, for which she was grateful, and at four, she gathered up her gifts and her things and left the office for home.

The weather had gotten considerably worse and it took the bus over an hour to move along the slick roads to his house. She was exhausted and sore by the time she kicked off her shoes and slipped out of her coat. Taking everything to the kitchen, she put on the kettle of water and went to change.

The wound on her thigh looked bad. It was hot to the touch and she could barely stand to have anything, including her flannel pants, touch it. Taylor was sure now that he may have broken the skin because there was something oozing from it and onto the padding she had put there before leaving for work. She took three pain killers and went to finish her tea and start her dinner.

At six, just sitting down to her fake dinner, as Jamie called it, the phone rang. She didn't answer it. No one knew she lived here but him and whoever he had told and they had yet to set up any kind of ground rules as to where that sort of stuff lay. When she heard his voice over the answering machine calling her name, she smiled and picked the receiver up.

"Oh, Jamie, you are so wonderful. You couldn't have picked a better thing to pick me up with."

"Hey, kiddo, are you having a rough day? Those bastards you...why don't you try and find another job, maybe after this weekend? I'll help you."

"I think you might be right. I don't think this one is going anywhere." She looked over at her backpack and thought about the files in it.

She hadn't taken them out, nor had she erased the thumb drive. Something wasn't right and she knew it. Whether or not she did anything about it...well, that was a different matter altogether. It took her several seconds to realize he was saying something.

"...due in June. Mom is over the moon with happiness. And Meggie is so excited about having a little sister than she is about to bust."

"I'm so happy for them. Jamie, are you sure about me and this dinner thing? I mean, I'm not exactly the rich and famous type of person, more of a beer and pizza kinda girl. And your family, what do they think about you bringing a nobody with you?" As soon as she said it, she knew that she shouldn't have.

"You're my friend, Taylor, and I won't have anyone, not even you, putting yourself down. Now. Is your dinner ready? We are about to say grace and I'm going to bring you along with us."

She could hear everyone being seated and the children talking excitedly. Taylor could hear Jamie talking and, also, she recognized his brother Byron. Her stomach hummed with the sound of his voice and that surprised her more than anything.

The man was gorgeous. His hair was a darker brown than Jamie's and saying it was brown was like saying that she was a girl. There were colors that defied description, and it curled ever so slightly at the ends. He had a classic face, long nose, heavy jaw, and full, pouty lips that didn't make him look feminine in the least. His pierced tongue had surprised her, but the diamond stud in his ear didn't. He was taller than Jamie's six-foot-four by probably another two inches and he was bulkier, more muscular across his chest. She knew he was a potter and figured that was why—all the upper body movements. When he had invaded her bedroom, his dark t-shirt was tucked into faded jeans that looked as if he had been melted down and poured like hot sex into them. Taylor wondered if his chest was smooth and what color his nipples were. The tear at the knee of his pants and the other on his thigh were not a product of style, she was sure, but of a man who worked at living and lived to play.

"Okay, everyone, tell Taylor happy Thanksgiving and I'll be right back." The entire family yelling to the phone had her smile and then it was quite. She assumed that he left the room.

"Are you okay, sweetie? I mean with this charity thing? I don't want you to go if you don't feel comfortable."

Tears prickled her eyes and she closed them. "I'm fine, I promise. I just...you know how I am with strangers. Promise you won't leave my side and I won't embarrass you overly much, all right?"

"Never. I'll stick to you like glue. I'll pick you up at six and don't eat much. There will be tons of food and decadent desserts. Love you, Ta. I'll see you tomorrow night."

"Love you too. Night."

Chapter Three

Byron couldn't stop thinking about the woman living with his brother. The marks on her back, the way she looked, and the way she had felt for those few fleeting moments when he had fallen into her arms had him wanting to drive back to Columbus and hunt her down. His cock had been near bursting for two days and he wanted relief. He knew of two clubs near his mother's house on the north side of Columbus, had even called them to see if they were open tonight, which surprisingly, they were. But he couldn't make himself go there. He wanted the little firebrand.

After stepping out onto the deck to cool off, he closed his eyes and thought about her. Taylor Bennett was a classic beauty from the top of her dark head of hair to the bottom of her feet. When she had stood in front of him, the towel draped over her breast, and her backside open to his view, he noticed the two dimples at the top of each cheek of her ass and salivated again at the thought of licking them. He thought there was a tattoo, but he couldn't be sure if it was a bruise or not. He couldn't wait to find out. Her ass was tight and full, and curved down to her sculptured thighs and muscled calves. When he had looked into her face, wide blue eyes stared back at him and he could almost feel the heat from her anger still when she had glared at him. Full lips, moist from the steam of the bath, beckoned his mouth to cover them, devour them. Byron knew that her breasts were real, large and firm. When he had fallen against her, he had felt the natural bounce to them and had wanted to throw his brother out and break down the door when she had locked him out.

He had never had a reaction to a woman this way before. He had wanted them and usually never had problems getting what he wanted, but this woman was different. He didn't want to think about what it could mean, but he was willing to play for a while. When he heard the door open to the deck and his brother Nicky stepped out, Byron actually groaned.

"That bad huh? Who is she and how much of a background check do you want me to run on her?" Nicky smiled.

"None, and it's not like that. She's...keep this to yourself, but she's Jamie's roommate. Christ, I only met her and she already has me in knots."

"Roommate? Wow! Do you think Mom knows? Well, that was a stupid question. He's still alive, isn't he? He must really like this girl—wait! You! Holy Christ, Byr, you're hitting Jamie's girlfriend?"

"No! Shit, no. He says they're just friends and that she is having some money issues. I think I believe him. But you should see this girl. Tall, dark hair, and a mouth that makes you think of sin and sex in a heartbeat. I don't even like her; she called me a barbarian, for crying out loud. Don't!" He knew as sure as he was standing there that Nicky was going to agree about the name, but didn't want to have to hurt him for it.

"Okay, for now anyway. Jamie said she's his date tomorrow night. Maybe you can charm her with your suaveness and impress her into liking you. It's happened before." Byron nodded, not really holding out much hope. She really didn't like him.

Byron glanced at his brother and thought about the other time he'd done a background check on a girl Byr was seeing. Antonia Clay had been perfect. Good background, moneyed and well-mannered when it counted. His mother had taken one look at her and hated her. The feelings were mutual. He chuckled. That was an understatement.

Spencer had just gotten married and so had Nick, to his first wife. Damon was engaged. So one quick weekend in Vegas and he had ended up married to the bitch from hell. She had been all right at first, civil to his family and tolerant of Meggie when she was born. It wasn't until Spencer got divorced a few years later that he realized that the women liked each other. They both couldn't

24

remain faithful if their lives had depended on it. When she had been caught for the eighth or ninth time with a man in a hotel room, he'd filed for divorce. The pre-nup was the only thing that had saved him from losing everything. He was more careful of his heart and his money.

~~~

Taylor woke at dawn throwing up. She was freezing one minute and burning up the next. And she ached. Calling off was out of the question, but she did call and make an appointment at the clinic. Luckily, her friend Angel said if she came in right now, she could look at her.

"You have a fever of a hundred and two and you're dehydrated. I think you have the flu. But without further testing, I can't say for sure. You need to go home and go to bed. Is your throat sore, how about your ears?" Angel asked as she took Taylor's blood pressure.

"Yeah, I pretty much ache everywhere. My head feels like I have someone in there directing a polka; my ears feel like if I could get something in there to scratch really hard, I'd feel better. My throat doesn't hurt so much as if feels dry and scratchy. I can't have the flu. I have a date tonight."

"Hummm, maybe you should cancel. I'm sure if he took one look at you, he'd understand. Oh! The charity thing with Jamie — I forgot about that. Honey, you'll be lucky if you make it through the day, much less this gala thing."

"Can't you give me something? I can't do this to him. He said that when one of his brothers fails to bring a date, their mother makes them spend untold amounts of money and sucking up to get back in her good graces. Besides, he's letting me rent a room from him for practically nothing."

"From what I've heard, the Grants can afford it. All right, I'll give you some antibiotic and something for the fever, but no drinking. And try to rest as much as you can today. And promise me that you'll come to see me on Monday if you aren't any better."

Taylor left and filled her prescription on the way to work. By the time the bus dropped her off in front of the building, she was ready to take a long nap. Dragging herself inside, she was greeted by a very cold room and no power. This couldn't be happening. She called the power company.

She called the Freedoms and told them that the power was off due to unpaid billing. She explained that they would need to pay the three oldest bills and a deposit before the power company would even consider coming out on Monday to turn things back on. They would also need to make arrangements to pay the other four bills that they were behind on.

Before she hung up with them, they had told her to take the day off without pay, of course, and that she was now in charge of keeping the power on. She was already in charge of the phone and gas, and the only reason those utilities stayed on. She called the answering service and gave them the Freedoms numbers, and went home. She was nearly giddy with relief when she got to her bed and crawled under the covers. The last thing she did before closing her eyes was set the alarm.

At two o'clock, she rolled out of bed and fell to the floor. Her leg was throbbing and was so sore she could barely stand up. Making it to the bathroom, she turned on the shower as hot as it would go and stepped in. She still couldn't touch the bite mark, and not just the bite but her entire thigh now. It was swollen and sore and the seepage was getting worst. She didn't tell Angel about it, fear and embarrassment making her keep her mouth shut. But Taylor was hoping that whatever was wrong with her had nothing to do with that and everything to do with the stress she was under. Angel had taken out the stitches from her arm while she was there as well.

After ten minutes of standing under the hot water, her leg and her body felt considerably better, the stiffness was nearly gone, and her head no longer hurt. Scrubbing every part of her body, shaving her long legs, and putting a deep conditioner on her hair, she actually felt human again. Humming a Christmas tune, she started to brush out her hair.

At most, her hair was curly, at its worst, it was a mop. She had threatened to cut it off several times over the past five years, but Jamie had told her that he liked it and if she cut it, he would be disappointed. She tried pointing out that he had cut his hair and he said it was because, as a teacher, he needed to set a good example. She had snorted at him.

By four, she was nearly dressed except for the actual dress itself. She had had it dry cleaned and pressed and she didn't want to wrinkle it. Pulling on her terry robe, she went to the kitchen to eat a little something. She still had no appetite and only ended up eating an apple. At five, she went up to pull on the dress and wait for Jamie.

She was coming back down when she heard his voice over the answering machine. Limping to the kitchen, she answered. While she had been upstairs putting the finishing touches on her hair and makeup, she started feeling bad again.

"Hey, the roads are really bad here and I've asked my brother and his wife to pick you up. He had a really nice SUV with four wheel drive. You'll like them; it's Devin and his wife Ronnie. Ronnie is about to pop out a kid in a few more weeks and is really weepy, so if she starts to cry, just hand her a tissue and let her go."

"Jamie, why don't I just take a cab? I don't...I don't like strangers, and this will make it..." The doorbell rang as she was trying to get out of riding with his brother.

"That'll be them. I knew you wouldn't want to ride with them, so I asked them to call when they were in the driveway. I promise, I'll be right here when you arrive. They know that you're shy. It'll be fine. I'll see you in about an hour."

He hung up before she could say anything else and she walked to the door. He was so going to pay for this when she saw him. Opening the door, she nearly slammed it shut again before she realized that it wasn't Byron, but another brother of Jamie's. Christ, had their mother made a pact with someone to have the most gorgeous men ever born?

"Ms. Bennett? I'm Devin Grant, Jamie's brother. I'm sorry about this, but Jamie insisted that given much more notice than this, you'd drive yourself rather than want us to pick you up. My wife is in the car. I didn't want her to fall. Shall we?"

He held her arm for her as they walked to the car. She hadn't realized that the weather had turned so bad and wondered if this was a good idea anyway. Devin opened the back door of his car for her and she slipped in. A very pregnant woman was on the seat next to her.

"I can't ride in the front because of the airbags. Not to mention my husband thinks that I won't fit up there anymore. I'm Ronnie Grant, you must be Taylor. This is going to be so much fun. I can't tell you how excited we've all been to meet you. And to think, he's had you hidden away for five years without letting us know about you."

"Jamie and I aren't a couple. We're just good friends and we're helping each other out. There is nothing going on between us," Taylor told the woman. She didn't want anyone getting the wrong impression about their relationship. She was uncomfortable enough about the social differences with them without his family thinking she was some sort of gold digger.

"Oh, I believe you. But just a heads up, don't tell his mother that you're living with him. She's really sweet, but very old fashioned, and she would probably snatch him bald if she knew."

Jamie had told her basically the same thing. His mother was wonderful and didn't want to think of her sons as having sex, he thought. He had told her that his mother, while very wonderful, was just plain scary when she was mad.

"Okay, but I'm not having sex with him. He's my friend and nothing more. The thought of having sex with him is just creepy." The laughter from the front seat reminded her that Devin was up there and listening to every word they said in the back.

"I bet a lot of women think that. Hell, the thought of Jamie being old enough to even think of having sex is still hard for me to believe. To me, he will always be the baby of the family and never a grown man."

The drive passed pleasantly enough. Ronnie was funny and had a wicked sense of humor, and she could cut her husband quick with her sharp tongue. Taylor felt herself relax by degrees and hoped that the rest of his family was just as nice.

The large, open area was decorated like a Santa workshop. Ronnie had told her that the trees had been decorated by florist around the area were being auctioned off too. Taylor couldn't imagine having one of the lavishly decorated trees in a house.

The first tree that greeted them was covered in small wooden toys — dolls, trains, cars and little drum sets. The twinkling lights, bright and shiny, bounced off the tinsel and made the tree seem alive. The red balls along with the red ribbons gave the tree the added color. The tree next to it had gingerbread men and women dressed in icing and ribbons. Taylor could almost smell the ginger and spices emanating from the tree, the cookies warmed by the lights on the tree and the room.

Each tree that they passed had a placard that told where it had come from and what company had decorated it. Some of the signs gave a list of the ornaments and the gifts, if any, accompanied the tree when sold. No wonder this auction made so much money. Someone had worked very hard on setting this all up. Taylor had said as much to Ronnie as they were being seated. Jamie grabbed her from behind before she could answer.

"Hello, beautiful," he said as she tumbled back into the chair. Pain radiated from her leg, and a whimper escaped before she could stop it. Taylor tried to hide it with a small laugh, and may have fooled everyone at the table but the woman sitting next to her.

"You all right? You look a little pale." Ronnie had introduced her as Caitlynne Grant, Spencer's new wife and the new mother-to-be.

Taylor knew that she was a homicide detective, O'Malley, as everyone had called her, and that Spencer's little girl, Meggie, was deaf. Spencer was a professor at the university and had just been named head of his department.

"I'm fine. Just a little overwhelmed. It's a lot to take in." Taylor didn't like the way O'Malley looked at her, but Byron chose that moment to sit down too — right next to her.

"Hello, Taylor. How are things today? Better?" She knew what he meant and decided to ignore his pointed question. For some reason she couldn't figure, he made her feel...wet.

"I'm fine, Mr. Grant. How are things with you? Break into anyone's house lately? Or is it just bedrooms you steal into?" And that was another thing; he brought out the snarkiness in her faster than anyone she knew.

Instead of being mad at her, he threw back his head and laughed. Her entire body tensed with need. And if she hadn't had a chill right then, she was sure she would have done something really embarrassing and asked him to laugh again just for the feeling he invoked in her body.

Dinner was served almost immediately. She had asked for the chicken dinner when Jamie had ordered for her and she found that she couldn't eat. Her throat was beginning to ache again and her head was starting to pound. She was sure that Jamie was getting tired of helping her put her shawl on and off again every ten minutes, but she just couldn't help it. As soon as the plates were cleared, the band started, and Taylor was ready to drop.

"Would you care to dance, Ms Bennett?" She was so startled by the request that all she could do was stare at Byron for several seconds before she realized he was talking to her.

"No! I mean, no. I...I'm with Jamie. Besides, I don't dance all that well. Thank you though." Her body felt on fire and not just from the man sitting next to her. Taylor wanted to strip off all her clothes and go out and dive into the nearest snow bank.

"Go ahead, Ta. Byr is a very good dancer. You know you love to dance." She turned to glare at Jamie, but he was playing with little Meggie and the little boys of Nick's and Morgan's, and didn't notice her dismay.

Byron stood and put out his hand. She could either cause a scene and refuse it, or she could just accept it and dance a small dance with him. To be honest, she did love to dance and would have loved to get out on the floor, but she wasn't sure that she could stand up for that long.

Standing, she staggered slightly. The room spun around quickly, but righted once, she put her hand in his. Taylor almost missed grabbing the back of her chair because she wasn't sure which one to pick as three swam in and out of focus for a second or two.

Before she knew it, she was on the dance floor with Byron's arms around her waist holding her up.

Chapter Four

"I don't feel so well," Taylor whimpered as she leaned against him. Byron had to agree that she didn't look so well either. He put his arms around her and pulled her tight against him so that he could whisper in her ear.

"Are you pregnant, Taylor?" Her body stiffened at his question and she stamped hard onto his foot. When she didn't apologize, he knew for sure that she did it on purpose. He continued with his queries. "I'll take that as a no. What's wrong? You're a green as that tree over there and about as sweaty as a man baling hay in deep July."

"You are such a charmer aren't you, dick head? I bet women just fall at your feet when you compare them to trees and sweaty men. It's a small wonder that you're not married." He smiled. There wasn't anything wrong with her wit. His concern shifted when she swayed in his arms and fell against him.

"Taylor!" And in the next instance, she went limp in his arms.

Looking at his table where his family was, he nodded to O'Malley and headed to the bathrooms. He wanted to get her out of the room and somewhere he could lay her down. He laid his cheek against her forehead and was amazed at the heat he felt there. Christ, she was burning up.

Cait, right on his heels, followed him into the ladies room and moved two chairs together to lay Taylor across. Thankfully, there was no one in the room and he knelt down beside her.

"I'll get Damon. Wet a few cloths and put them over her forehead. Damn it, I knew there was something wrong the moment she sat down. I'll be right back." Suddenly, he was alone with her.

He wanted to cuddle her in his arms and hold her and was amazed at the notion. He was neither a cuddlier nor did she strike him as one. He smiled when he thought about how she would tear a strip off his hide in a heartbeat if he were to even suggest such a thing. Byron's mother and Damon rushed in a minute or two later.

"What's wrong? Christ, she's burning up. Byron, go get my bag from the coat area and I'll examine her."

"No. I'm not leaving her. I'll have Jamie get it, but I'm staying." He didn't look at his mother's face, but he felt her gaze. Byron didn't know himself why he needed to stay with her.

Taylor's eyes suddenly popped open. Byron let go of the breath he hadn't realized he was holding. She looked right at him and whimpered.

"Taylor, you have a high grade fever. Can you tell me what else is wrong? Have you been throwing up, chilled? Have you eaten anything today?" Damon asked her as he checked her pulse. He shook his head at Byron when he started to ask. That couldn't be good.

"I'm fine. Really, let me up. I don't know what came over me. I guess it was all the excitement of the day."

"Taylor, this is not excitement. You have a fever. I'm thinking some sort of infection is running throughout your system and I can't treat it if I don't know what it's from," Damon said to her in his "I'm the doctor" voice.

Her face flushed and with a quick glance at him, Byron knew, or at least he had a good idea. One of the marks, the raw ones on her back, had gotten infected. He needed to ask her, but not in front of his family.

"Damon, Mom, can you give me a few minutes? I think I can clear this up. I won't be long."

His mother looked like she wanted to say something, but thought better of it and left. Damon was a little harder to convince. He finally left the room, but wasn't happy about it. Byron turned to Taylor.

"The other day when I saw you, I told you there were raw places on your back. One of them is infected, isn't it? If you had just let me see them..."

"No, my back is fine. And it's also none of your business. Let me up. I'm going to call a cab and..." Her scream startled them.

Byron had leaned on her legs to keep her from standing and hurt her somehow. His brother Jamie came rushing back into the room and nearly knocked Byron over to see what he had done. Looking down, he could see that her right thigh was swollen, her dress stretched tight over it.

"Let me see your leg, Taylor." She started shaking her head and trying to stand. He pressed her back against the chair and leaned on her shoulders. "Show us your leg, or so help me, I will punish you." He had used his Dom voice and knew if she were a true Sub, she would have no choice but to obey. He heard Jamie hiss at him, but before he could say anything, Taylor started talking to their brother Damon when he came back into the room.

"It's nothing. Please, I beg you; don't make me do this, please."

"Now! Your punishment is now twice as bad, shall we go for three? Show us," he demanded harshly.

Dropping her eyes, Taylor whimpered. "I can't reach it, master. I hurt."

Byron reached the bottom of the dress at the hem and pulled the material apart. He never took his eyes from hers once the dress started to peel open.

"Byron, what the hell are you doing? Taylor is...holy mother of God," Jamie finished on a whisper.

Byron glanced down. Teeth marks. Someone had bitten her and bitten her hard. The red streaks running up her leg couldn't be good, and a quick look at Damon confirmed that. She was shaking again and he slipped off his jacket and laid it over her. Jamie looked at Taylor and backed away, his face as pale as hers.

"Mom." Damon shouted at her as she stood in the doorway. "Call an ambulance. We need to get her to a hospital right away." Taylor fainted again.

Byron sat on the floor of the bathroom, watching her, and he didn't say a word. He really didn't know what he could say. No one had asked him how he knew that Taylor had been hurt nor did anyone question him about the tone he had used on her to get her to obey him. He knew that they had questions. Hell, so did he.

He glanced over at Jamie who stood in the doorway. As soon as he realized that the marks on Taylor's leg were teeth marks, he had moved to the other side of the room and not said a word. Byron could imagine what was going through Jamie's head—how, who, when, why and shit. Byron didn't have any answers for him, none that he would share until he talked to Taylor, at least. Caitlynne, however, had plenty to say.

"When we get her to the hospital, I have an officer there waiting to take pictures. Whoever did this to her was working beyond the normal BDSM scope. I would never have pegged her as a submissive, would you?" He knew she was fishing; she had been standing outside the door when he had threatened Taylor. He didn't say anything. Nodding, she continued.

"Don't you people have safe words you use? I mean, a bite that hard, she would have been in a great deal of pain when he did it. I wonder why she let him...unless she wanted him to...Nah, I don't think that's it, do you, Byron?" He looked at her now.

"I can't answer anything you're asking me. Whatever happened to her happened before I met her. Yes, she's a Sub. How deep, I have no idea."

"You know a great deal about this type of thing thought, don't you, Byr? I can understand why you won't say anything about her injuries, but you do know what could have happened."

"I'm not a submissive, if that's what you're implying. Leave off, Cait. I told you all I'm going to tell you without her permission."

~~~

Taylor woke to a dark room. She didn't have any idea where she was. The last thing she remembered, she was at the charity thing with Jamie and she had been dancing with Byron. Sitting up suddenly, she remembered him telling her he was going to punish her and pain ripped through her. She laid back and breathed through her nose and out her mouth as she tried to control the pain in her leg as it shot through her body. Moving her arm, she felt the IV and realized she was in the hospital. Moving her hand through the bed, she came up with the call button and the large electronic thing that controlled everything else in the room. Trying to find the light, she pushed buttons. The TV came on first, then off, then suddenly she was moving up, and then down. About ready to give up and pull the stupid chain, the light suddenly flared on behind her.

The room was huge and very nice. She knew it had to be a private only because she had been in the hospital before and with her insurance, she was lucky that they didn't put her in the hall and leave her there. There was no way she could afford this. There was a big screen television and a beautiful couch, not the kind that was so uncomfortable that you would feel better on the floor than to sleep on it, but one that she thought could grace any nice house. There was the usual stuff that went with hospital rooms, as well, the bed she was in and a chair and computer. Looking over to the wall, she found a small closet and hoped that her clothes were there. There were two nice bunches of flowers, but she couldn't see who they were from, and a telephone, pitcher, and glass.

Taylor pulled the sheet back and looked at her leg. It was bandaged nicely and neatly. It didn't hurt anyway near as bad as it had and it felt cooler to the touch. Wiggling her toes, she realized, while sore, she could move the muscle without causing the ripping pain she had had before. Before she could continue her inventory of her body, the door opened and a nurse stepped in.

"Well, hello there. I didn't know you had awakened yet. Dr. Grant said you'd probably be out until tomorrow sometime. Is there anything I can get you? You can have some light dinner if you want. The kitchen is closed, but I can get you something light if you're hungry."

"Yes, that's great. What time is it? And the date, please." She thought she could get someone to come and get her if it wasn't too late.

"It's just after nine on Sunday evening. You've been here for about two days. Let me get you your dinner ordered and then I'll come back and get your blood pressure and such."

The nurse was only gone a few minutes before she returned. She told Taylor that it would be about twenty minutes for her food and then she started wrapping up her arm in the blue cuff.

"I was wondering if I could call my friend, please? If you'd just hand me the phone, I'd appreciate it." Taylor wanted to go home; she couldn't afford to rake up a high bill.

When the nurse handed her the phone and told her how to dial out, Taylor called Jamie. He answered on the first ring.

"Hey! It's Taylor. How's it going?" The nurse went into the bathroom. Taylor realized that Jamie hadn't said anything after saying his name.

"Yeah. I'm...what do you want, Taylor? I'm really busy." His voice sounded hard and upset.

"I was wondering if you could come and..."

"Look, I think it was a mistake you moving in here. When you get out, I'll help you find a place to live. But right now, I've...I'll talk to you some other time." And the phone went dead.

Taylor sat there in stunned silence. Jamie didn't want her there anymore. Looking down at her leg, she realized that whoever had brought her here must have realized that the wound was caused by teeth marks and from there figured out what she was. The nurse must have said something to her and it wasn't until she took the dead phone from her that Taylor heard her.

"Are you all right, honey? You look like you've seen a ghost or something. Want me to call the doctor for you?"

"No. No, I'm all right. I've...he said that...do you think I could please be alone? I'm suddenly very tired."

The nurse left a few minutes later and Taylor sank back down into the bed. She wanted to cry, to throw something or scream, but knew that it would do her no good. Jamie hated her. He had finally found out what she was and now he didn't want anything to do with her. Looking over at the little bunch of daisies on the table, she was suddenly sick. Pulling the cord again, the nurse came flying back in the room.

Chapter Five

At eight the next morning, Byron walked into Taylor's room. He was surprised to see the bed empty and started to go to the desk to find out where she had gone when he heard the toilet flush. Taylor came out slowly and he could tell she had been crying.

"Let me help..."

"Stay away from me. I've got it." Anger was evident in her voice, which was harsh and unforgiving. He didn't move back, but Byron didn't touch her either.

Thinking she was going back to the bed, he went there ahead of her to help her back into it and was surprised to turn and find her in sitting in one of the chairs. The chair was on wheels and she was pushing herself with her feet over to the window.

The snow had started again early this morning and the streets were getting traitorous. It had taken him more than an hour to travois the normally twenty minute drive to the hospital. There had been lots of vehicles on the side of the road and a couple of fender benders. He sat in the other chair and watched her.

She wouldn't look at him, but he was fine with that. She was more than likely embarrassed about the other night. He knew that he would be. Cait had called him earlier and asked him to meet her there to talk with Taylor in the event of Cait having questions about anything that might have happened that she didn't understand.

"Taylor, Caitlynne, my sister-in-law, is coming in to talk to you this morning. She is going to ask you questions about the wound on your leg. I didn't tell her anything, but she is a good detective and she figured out a great deal on her own. Can you tell me where you were when you got bit?"

Nothing. Taylor didn't move, but continued to stare out the window. He noticed that she had closed her eyes and a tear fell along her cheek. As a Dom he wouldn't tolerate tears, but right now, he wasn't anything more to her than a brother of the man she lived with. She had no reason to trust him, or for that matter, like him.

"Taylor, look at me and tell me what you're thinking. If it's about your wound, it'll heal fine. It was infected, probably from an infection he may have had in his mouth—Damon said a cavity more than likely." She sighed, but still didn't say anything, and then Cait walked in.

Byron liked his sister-in-law, all three of them, as a matter of fact. But honestly, Cait intimidated him somewhat. He wasn't sure if it was the fact that she carried a gun for a living or that she was just so brave and gutsy. She had once killed seven men to save Spencer's little girl. She had done it with a bullet hole in her leg and a severe concussion. Yeah, he thought, she was all that.

"Hello, Taylor. I don't know if you remember me, but I'm Detective Grant. I'm Jamie and Byron's sister-in-law. I have a few questions I'd like to talk to you—"

"I'll answer them, but just you. He needs to leave." She didn't open her eyes. Her voice was low and cold.

Byron looked over at Cait and stood to leave when she nodded to him. "I have a few questions of my own when she is finished, Taylor. I'll be right outside."

His phone was ringing when he sat in the lobby down from Taylor's room. He pulled it out and answered before he looked to see who it was.

"You aren't at the airport. Damn it, Mr. Grant, do you know how hard it is to get you to shows if you don't at least leave to get there? You're supposed to be in Paris on Tuesday morning, not in Ohio on Monday morning."

Shit, he forgot. What with everything going on, he forgot about the exhibit and sale of his work in France that would run for two weeks straight. It was a charity event that had been planned last fall and he had to go.

"I'm leaving right now to go to the airport. I'll need you to have...never mind, I'll get what I need there. Call the hotel and tell them that I'll be there and not to give up my room, please." He was moving to the nurse's station as he talked.

"Clothes are already in the plane. All the information you need, including the itinerary, is there as well. The jet is ready as soon as you get your ass buckled in."

Some days, like today, he didn't care much for his assistant, but he always got the job done and made sure that everything was just the way Byron liked it. He thought he should make sure the kid got a raise and made a mental note to call his brother. Nicky would bitch about the money, but hell, it was his and he could afford it.

After scribbling a quick note to say what happened, he left the hospital and headed toward the airport. He would call Jamie or Cait later tonight and see how the interview went.

~~~

Cait sat in the chair that Byron had just vacated. She was actually nervous about asking the young girl questions. Cait knew much more about her and her lifestyle than she had before, thanks to the Internet.

"Taylor, I'd like to ask you—"

"Whatever I say to you, it's just between us, correct? I mean, I know that the Grants are your family, but you don't run home and tell them anything, do you?"

Cait supposed she could have been insulted, but she wasn't. Taylor didn't know her or anything about her so she simply answered her truthfully. She wasn't so stupid to think that Spencer wouldn't ask, but she wouldn't tell him anything.

"No, everything you say to me is confidential, unless it goes to trial. That would be up to you, though. If you wanted to press charges against the man who bit you, it is perfectly within your rights. It's a bad bite, Taylor, and it could have been very serious if Damon hadn't been there to treat you for it. I understand that you people have safe words. Did you want him to hurt you this bad?"

Cait watched Taylor for any reaction, anything, but the girl just sat there. Her eyes were still closed, but there were more tears on her cheeks. Cait was very good at reading people and she could get nothing from Taylor at all.

"He...I didn't want him to bite me. When my sort of people go to a club, the first—"

"Taylor, I'm sorry. I didn't mean to say—" Cait wanted to take back what she had said; she never meant it the way Taylor had obviously taken it. But she cut her off before she could explain.

"When we first go to a club, we fill out a sheet telling them what we want, what can be used, and the amount of pain we think we can tolerate. And yes, I have a safe word. That's on the sheet as well. He wouldn't...it didn't matter to him. He wouldn't stop."

"Did he hear you say it? And how many times did you have to say it before he stopped?" Cait was complying a list of things to look up when she got back to the office. Since Taylor had taken Byron out of the picture, she would have to get her answers elsewhere.

"I said my word eighteen times before I passed out from the pain. And he stopped, I was told, when he came. I'm very tired now, Detective. I'd like for you to leave."

Cait sat there, stunned. Taking advantage of someone, even in a club setting such as Taylor had been in, was rape. If what Taylor was telling her was true, and Cait had no doubt that it was, then Taylor had been raped as surely as if it had happened in a dark alley.

"Taylor, if you tell me where this occurred and who it was that did it, I'll bring him in for questioning. I'm sure that Devin could take him to trial and have him up on rape charges so fast that his head would spin. What he did to you was wrong."

The laughter that spilled from Taylor's mouth startled Cait. The sound, brittle and manic, made the hair on her arms stand up. And the fact that she hadn't moved made it seem all the more eerie.

"No, Detective. I'm not pressing charges. Please go away. I'm very tired. Could you please tell Mr. Grant that I'm not up to speaking to him? I'd really appreciate it." Taylor slowly got to her feet and shuffled her way to the bathroom and closed the door.

Cait stood as well and looked down at her notes. The word rape was there in the margin, as well as in her notes, but without dragging Taylor into the station and trying to get her to press charges; she would have nothing to hold the man on. Not yet anyway. Eighteen times she had said her safe word and then

Taylor had passed out from pain. Shaking her head, Cait left the poor girl alone. But she did go to the two clubs in town to see if they would let her see the recording of the event if there was one. She hit pay dirt on the first try with the "Flogger."

Chapter Six

Taylor pulled the towel off the counter, put it over her mouth, and screamed into it. Tears streamed down her face as she sobbed. Her heart ached and she didn't think she could stand too much more. She sat there for a while, not really caring if Cait left or not.

She had taken her bag into the bath earlier, but when she heard the door open to the room, she stepped out to find Byron there and was glad that she hadn't changed. Pulling her bag out of the curtained tub, she began the process of putting on her jeans and t-shirt.

Taylor had called her friend Angel at six-thirty that morning and had made arrangements for her to pick her up this afternoon. Angel had gone by Jamie's house and gotten Taylor's bag of clothes for her and had given Jamie the key back. He hadn't said a single word to her after she told him what she was there for. Angel had dropped off the clothes Taylor was putting on just before Byron came in. When Taylor was dressed, she hobbled back into the room and called Angel again.

"Are you sure this is a good idea? I mean, you can stay with me for a couple of days. At least until you can get around enough to walk without too much pain. I've already cleared it with my husband and he's fine with it," Angel asked when Taylor told her it was time.

"No thanks. I just need a ride to the Y and that's all. I've already called them and they are holding a room for me. Betsey works there and she said that she'd hold it until noon. Besides, I need to go to work tomorrow. The Freedoms aren't very happy with me already. And I can't afford to miss any more work."

Angel tried for a few more minutes, but Taylor had her mind set. It wasn't just the job or the room; she just didn't want to see any more people right now, including the Grants. Fifteen minutes later, Angel walked in with the AMA papers that Taylor needed to leave without the doctor's permission. "Against Medical Advice" meant that Taylor couldn't sue the hospital if something happened to her after she left, but she really didn't care one way or the other if it did.

The nurses put up a huge fuss and threatened Taylor with calling back in Detective Grant. When that failed, they said they would call Mrs. Parker and Doctor Damon Grant. In the end, Taylor walked out as the head nurse was dialing the phone to Damon's office.

Her room at the Y was nice, small but clean. Taylor didn't have a television, but then she seldom watched it. She loved music, but she had enough tunes on her computer that it was no problem hooking in the ear buds and listening to them for a while, so she didn't miss the radio. There was a single bed and a dresser, and after putting her things in it, she laid down. She really was tired and her leg throbbed. She supposed she should eat, but wasn't hungry. On her way home from work tomorrow, she decided that she would go to the store and pick up some fruit and a few snacks.

Taylor thought about what Cait had said. "You people," she had said. As if she was a different sort of person than a human. Taylor wondered if that's what Jamie thought, that she was a subhuman.

She had heard it before—sexual deviant, sadist, sick. She supposed in a way she was. She didn't choose her sexual preference; it sort of chose her. Smiling, she thought that that wasn't a true statement either, because Taylor had never had sex. She had gotten off, had some incredible climaxes, and had been responsible for a few of them, too, in her partners, but she had never allowed anyone to enter her. She wasn't into this for the sex, but for the release, the sated feeling she got from it. But she was done with it. As soon as she was able, she was moving back to her home state of Florida and seeing about getting back into the club she had started at.

She had been a waitress there. She had just turned twenty-one and needed a part-time job. The owner, Josh Milligan, a Dom, told her that he would give her a trial run. She had been working a month when he asked her if she wanted to work a party for him; he needed an extra waitress. She agreed. The money was great and she made great tips he said she could keep.

The party was in full swing when Josh came up behind her and took her tray. His body pressed over hers had made her wet and achy. She had been breathing hard all night, watching the others being tied down and whipped, and the need to join pressed on her hard.

"You like this don't you, Ta? You like to watch the flogger hit their skin, leave a mark. Are you wet? Do you want to spank them?"

Taylor shook her head and watched as another woman was tied to the St. Andrews Cross. She had been naked except for the collar around her throat and the blindfold over her eyes. The first time the man smacked his partner's bare bottom with his open hand, Josh ran his hand up under Taylor's skirt and squeezed her ass, his cock pressed hard against her hip.

"You're so wet, Ta, wet and hot. You want to be there? You want to be smacked like that, your ass all pink and burning? Answer me, Ta; don't make me have to ask you a second time."

"Yes, master. That's what I want. I want to feel the pain burning through me." The urge to call him "master" came naturally to Taylor, and Josh nipped at her neck as a reward.

"I want to do that to you. I want to tie you over that bench and beat your ass until you can't stand it. Will you let me, Ta? Will you be my Sub tonight?" He started moving them toward the padded bench. As he spoke to her, he unsnapped her jeans and worked the zipper down. Her body ached for things she didn't understand. She didn't know all the rules, but knew enough to understand that she would belong to him this one night if she agreed.

"Yes, master. Tonight. I don't...I don't know what I'm supposed to do." Josh pressed her down on the bench and strapped her hands to the straps on the floor. He grabbed her shirt, a tee with the bar's name on it, and ripped if from her back, leaving her bra intact. Next, he pulled her pants and panties down to her ankles and opened her legs. He adjusted the height of the bench so that her feet were braced on the floor and then he had buckled her ankles against the legs of the bench too.

Taylor was on fire. She no longer cared that there were about thirty people in the room. All she could see, all she could feel, was Josh. And think about, anticipate, what he was going to do to her.

"You can't come until I let you. If you do, then I will punish you. You can't scream until you ask me if you can. If you do, then I will punish you." He smacked her ass hard. "You will do what I tell you to do without question or I will punish you. The rest we will work out as we go. You need a safe word. Think about what you want it to be. Once you say it, everything stops and you leave. Oh, and Taylor, I will never enter you. I never have sex with my Subs. I will come on you and over you. I may even come down your throat, but never inside of you. Understand?" She was trying to figure out how that worked when he brought his hand down twice hard on her ass. "When I ask you something, you'll answer me."

"Yes, master."

"Good." And so her introduction to the world of pain and pleasure began. He had had to punish her only once in the two years they had been together. She had failed to make him come in less than two minutes once and he had denied her a climax for three days while they played. She never missed another deadline again.

When Josh had met Cybil, he didn't want to play at the club anymore with anyone but Cybil. Taylor was fine with that. Josh and Cybil were so happy together, and she, Cybil and Josh all parted on good terms. She still heard from them on occasion, Christmas cards and the occasional email, and was happy to find out they had finally gotten married and had a baby.

Taylor moved to Ohio soon after for reasons she still couldn't remember and had met Jamie a few days later. It made her hurt to think about him and she closed her eyes against the pain. She hoped him the best of luck in his life, she really did.

~~~

Byron was sitting in his hotel room, thinking about Taylor, and decided to call his brother Jamie. Even with thousands of miles separating him from her, Byron still wanted her.

"Hey, I just got back to the hotel room and wondered if you've seen Taylor today. She seem okay? I had to leave quickly and didn't explain. Cait was with her when I left."

"No, I've been busy today. I...I have to go, Byr. Call Cait. I'll see you." And the phone went dead.

To say that Byron was shocked would have been an understatement. His brothers and he were close and to have one of them practically hang up on him hurt. He sat there for several minutes trying to figure out what he had done and decided that his brother was more in love with Taylor than he had said. Byron felt badly for his involvement with Taylor at the Charity Ball, but he wouldn't change what he had done for anything. He called Cait next, but he got Spencer instead.

"Taylor checked herself out of the hospital right after Cait left. The nurse said they couldn't talk her into of staying no matter how much they threatened. Cait is taking it pretty bad. She seems to think she might have said something to her that might have hurt her. And before you ask, she won't tell you. I've been trying all day. She's lying down now."

"There seems to be a lot of that going around. Have you talked to Jamie? He practically hung up on me just now, told me that he was busy. What's going on with him?"

"Christ, I don't know. Mom called and said the same thing. She told me that she and Morgan had gone by the hospital to see Taylor and found out she was gone. They called Jamie and he told her Taylor wasn't his responsibility and that he didn't have any idea where she was nor did he care. Then he had the nerve to hang up on her. She was really pissed when she called here, then she started sobbing. Do you know how much it hurts to have your mom and your wife crying on your shoulder and there isn't a damned thing you can do to fix it?"

Byron had made his mom cry once, but he didn't have a wife anymore and never expected to get another one, so the other he didn't know. After the brothers commiserated for several more minutes about their woes in life, they hung up. Byron got up and sat at his computer and did some business then went to bed. He just hoped it paid off.

The Grant brothers were very wealthy men. Their grandfather, a self-made millionaire, had left each of them a legacy and a promise. They needed to work their way through college, graduate in the top of their class, and make something of themselves. And they had, not only meeting his expectations, but exceeding them by leaps and bounds.

Spencer had become a teacher straight out of college. He loved what he did and had become one of the most sought after professors at Ohio State. Recently, he had been promoted to the head of his department, gotten married, and would soon be a father again.

Damon had been a great surgeon as an open heart specialist. About seven years ago, he had given it all up and become a general practitioner and opened his own practice. He, too, worked in the Grant building.

Nickolas was a wiz at finance, and had made him and all of them richer because of it. He had met his wife Morgan when she had come into the office for an interview. He now had a set of twin boys that were perfect in every way.

Devin was a very good attorney. He and his wife Ronnie were having their first child any day now and the first baby girl in the family in a long time. Devin worked in the Grant building and helped out when any of them needed legal representation.

Jamie, the baby of the family, was also a teacher at Ohio State and had just been offered his tenureship. He had also just been made head of his department, taking over Spencer's position when he had left. Jamie also worked a great deal with the mentally handicapped and whenever he could, he got his brothers involved as well.

Byron was an artist. He had started out as an oil painter and now changed his medium over to clay. He had learned to throw on a wheel while in college and hadn't done anything with it until ten years ago when he decided to try painting on pottery pots. His work now graced the homes of some of the most famous people; the President had several pieces and there was rumor that the Queen herself had a piece or two lying around the castle. He also owned several businesses that he kept very close tabs on. One of which was a bondage club.

The opening of the club, "Tightly Bound," nine years ago had started out as a way for him and a couple other Doms he knew to get together and have some down time without anyone knowing who they were. It had worked out very well, both financially and sexually, for the men. Then about three years ago, his partners had decided to move on and had let Byron buy them out. He now had three others across the United States and visited them all at least three times a year.

"Tightly Bound" in Ohio was equipped with an office and his own play room. When he would come by to play, there was never any question of him finding a playmate for the night; it was finding just one. Byron, a sexual Dom, had built up his collection of toys over the years and had even had several pieces of hardware made and modified for his own personal use. And like most Doms, he gave his Subs a list to fill out of what they wanted and how much playtime they needed.

There had never been a time when he had gone too far with a Sub and when they said their safe word, everything stopped and the Sub went home. They were not banned from his place like most clubs, but if after three times they had to call a stop, they were asked not to return for an entire year. Most of them usually never returned, but those that did come back with a better handle on their needs usually worked out well.

Tonight, he sent an email to his manager and told him to notify Byron if anyone by the name of Taylor Bennett called or emailed requesting an invitation. Byron knew that Taylor was a true Sub or she wouldn't have obeyed him the night of the dance. He also hoped that she would need to find another place to visit soon and he wanted to know when she did.

The clubs he owned didn't just allow anyone to walk in off the streets. An invitation needed to be requested from the club, or someone already a member would issue them one. An extensive background check and a blood test were required before admittance was granted to keep out the drug addicts and criminals. Byron hoped that Taylor wouldn't go back to the one where she had been hurt, assuming, of course, that is what had happened, and would try and find another place soon. He just hoped she waited until he was back in the States before she ventured into his place.

Chapter Seven

Taylor pulled the thumb drive out of her computer and dated it. She was alone in the office again and didn't expect anyone to come in for the rest of the day. She was glad; she hurt in more places than she thought she had names for.

She had been back to work for a week now. And as it was Friday, she had two days off she could rest up for another week. Taylor wondered if she would be able to get rested enough in just two days, but knew that she had little to no choice. She needed the money.

The thing with the insurance companies bothered her every time she put a credit into the ledger. The Freedoms had emailed her on Monday that they wanted her to take over the accounting part of the business fully. They offered her an extra fifty bucks a payday and she eagerly accepted.

Jason had taken her to the bank that afternoon and had given her access to the company checking account and made sure that she could sign checks to pay the bills. The incident with the power being shut off had pissed them off and when she pointed out the unsigned checks on his desk, he blustered for two hours.

"From now on, you make sure the power stays on. I can't very well bring a client here to help him with his needs if I can't offer them a decent cup of coffee now, can I?" Taylor shook her head no, thinking that not having any lights should have been more of a problem, but said nothing.

Dropping the thumb drive into her bag, she thought about the safety deposit box she had opened yesterday to keep the drives. There were only three in there now — one on Thanksgiving Day and

51

the Thursday and Friday after her hospital stay, but with the five she had made this week, she was getting nervous.

At first, she was going to only copy the files onto a drive every other day and use three drives to do it. But she realized that there were major changes to the company accounts every day, large deposits and bigger withdrawals that she decided to make a copy of daily. On the third day, Friday, she was about to reuse the original drive when she noticed that it was time stamped and dated. Thinking that might be a good thing to have, she went to the store and purchased as many thumb drives as she could afford.

She smiled when she thought how she had gone all over Columbus one day, buying two here, another one there so that no one would get suspicious about why she was buying them up. She had no idea why she thought that was necessary, but had also kept the receipts to prove that she had paid for them and the date and time that she had done it. It was silly, she knew, but it had filled an entire otherwise boring evening for her.

She squirmed in her chair. She was getting achy again. She tried not to think about how much she needed to go to a club, but it seemed the more she tried not to think about it, the more she did. She had tried making herself come, but that hadn't worked. It had only made her more frustrated. Closing her eyes, she thought about Jamie's voice again to cool off.

She hadn't heard from him since that night. He had never called her to see if she was all right and she couldn't bring herself to call him. She thought he had made it perfectly clear that he no longer wanted anything to do with her. Taylor understood. She didn't like it, but she understood. There had been a message from Byron Grant, but she never returned his call and had deliberately deleted his number from the incoming call list.

She was putting in the last of the credits when she noticed something different. Her name. Someone had changed the name on the accounts she was working with to hers. Taylor looked at the amount going out of the account and then the name of the person authorizing the withdrawal and got dizzy.

Almost seven hundred thousand dollars had been removed from one of the insurance accounts and into an account with her name on it. Opening the account and pulling up the ledger from the bank, she could see where she, or at least someone saying they were her, had been doing this for over a year. With shaky hands, she called the bank.

"Oh yes, Ms. Bennett. I meant to call you. When the Freedoms gave you the access to the business accounts, that one wasn't put on the list for some reason. I figured it out yesterday and added it to your access. I was going to call you, but I completely forgot. Is there a problem with the account? I actually thought it was odd that you didn't already have access, but then realized that you probably didn't think you could link your account with theirs. I also have the account number to the other account as well. If you have a pen, I can give you that now."

Taylor wrote down the numbers and repeated them back to her twice. After assuring her that it was fine and that Taylor wasn't upset, the lady told Taylor how to access that account as well.

"I've not been here long, but I think that's an overseas account, right? The reason I ask is that my husband and I are thinking of opening up one of those Swiss accounts to put our IRA money into. I guess the taxes are much lower and there are no penalties for taking it out. Do you know much about them?"

"No, it's...it's, ahhhh...I had to search for the information online, and most of it made no sense to me, but I thought, what the heck, what can it hurt right?" Taylor was babbling and she closed her eyes to what she was saying.

She sounded like a ninny and needed to get off the phone before she said something really stupid like, "by the way, I think this money is being laundered through your bank and the men I work for are doing it."

Hanging up with the banker, she started to open the account and remembered something she had seen on the TV once. This person who owned a Swiss bank account had been notified when someone accidentally opened their account and had been murdered for it. Taylor decided that she was never watching another movie again unless there were copious amount of talking animals or it was a cartoon. She also decided she was in way over her head.

On the bus ride back to the Y, she tried to convince herself that she would just stop making copies of the books and simply go about her business. She wasn't sure what she would do, or even if she could do about the accounts in her name, though. By the time she got off the bus in front of the bank, she was no closer to figuring it out than she had before.

She put all but one of the drives in the drawer. She didn't know why she had kept today's drive out. But by the time she was back on the bus for the last leg of her journey, it was too late to return and put it in there as well. When she got to her room, she decided she needed someone to answer a few questions and went to the common room to use that computer. It had the Internet, which her laptop didn't when here. But she was stressed and antsy, and this time, thinking about Jamie didn't work.

Before she knew it, she was on the business yellow pages looking for another club. Just because she was looking didn't mean she was going to go, she thought. And thinking that made her feel marginally better. Doing a search brought up two names.

"The Flogger" was the one she had gone to and been hurt, so she mentally crossed that off her list. The only other one was "Tightly Bound." The full page ad said that they catered to a private atmosphere and that they had a long and impressive list of clients. Taylor snorted. That could mean they have three people on their list and no one else. She had tried to get a membership before, but they had a long waiting list. But she filled out the online application again. She got an immediate email back asking her to verify that she had sent a request in. She hovered over the "yes" tab for several seconds before she finally clicked it. Closing down the site for this search, she opened another, looking for someone to give her free advice. Twenty minutes later, halfway around the world, Byron got an email too.

That evening Taylor was sick with worry. The movie The Firm was on the television in the common room and, like an idiot, she had stayed up to watch it. At ten-thirty she was pacing the room and biting her nails. That was when she noticed the evening copy of the Columbus Dispatch.

Devin and Veronica Grant had given birth that morning—a baby girl. They were the lawyers in the Grant family. Ronnie had been really nice to her and she was the one who had given her the daisies in the hospital. She worried her thumb nail a little more

Byrd

then decided to call her. She knew it was late, but Taylor so didn't want to catch anyone else there when she called. Of course this would only work if she could get through to her, Taylor thought.

Surprisingly, the nurse asked her to hold on and the phone rang once more then Ronnie answered. Taylor almost hung up. Ronnie had been laughing at something when she had answered the phone, Taylor was sure, and didn't want to spoil that for her. But she was getting desperate.

"Mrs. Grant. It's Taylor Bennett. Please don't say anything. I just need to ask you a question and I promise I won't bother you again."

"It's lovely to hear from you again. I've been...Devin, honey, why don't you go get me a cola. I've not had one in nine months and I want one in the worst way." Taylor heard someone mumble something and then Ronnie's clear laughter again. "Yes. I have my lover on the phone and I want to talk sexy to him—go away." Several mores seconds passed and then Ronnie was back. "All right, Taylor. Where the hell are you? I've been trying to find you for over a week. My family has been worried sick over you. Are you all right?"

Taylor burst into tears. Not because the woman yelled at her, because she had—no. it was because she was the first person who had asked her that since she had been out of the hospital. It took her a full five minutes of crying before she felt under control enough to talk again.

"I'm sorry. It's been...I've been so stressed out and I just don't know what to do. I...please, Mrs. Grant, please don't say anything to anyone that I called. I can imagine what they think of me. I mean what with Jamie and all. I just needed some advice."

"First of all, don't call me Mrs. Grant. I'm Ronnie. And what do you mean about Jamie? Do you know what's wrong with him?"

Taylor didn't know what she meant so she launched into what she needed. She wasn't sure how far he would have to go for a cola, but was sure that Devin would be back shortly. It took her three tries, but she finally got it all out.

"I just need to know where I can go to look and see if I'm overreacting. I've been nervous for a few weeks that I'll get caught looking these things up, and not sure that if it is legal, then what

55

the Fre...my boss will do if he finds out what I've done." Taylor didn't want to give away her firm's name. It wasn't that she didn't want them to get into trouble so much as that she wanted to cover her own butt. Nor did she mention the copies or the thumb drives. She felt guilty enough.

"Sweetie, I haven't a clue what you're talking about. Take a deep breath and then start over, slowly. What is it you think is illegal? And just so you know, generally, if it feels illegal, it usually is."

"There are these insurance policies that they are collecting the interest off of. I've been noticing the same amounts being deposited into their account for a few weeks now. Can they do that?"

"Yes, of course. A lot of firms set up these accounts or have the customer set them up so that when they die, there is some money they can use to pay the firm's legal fees. I've seen a couple of them exceed the amount of the policy and then it goes into the estate at the time of death," Ronnie said.

"Yeah, but if their dead, what then?"

"Well, then the next firm would take the monies and do the same thing. There is usually a waiver in the policy in case that happens. But normally, the lawyer's estate will take care of that."

"No, I mean what if the policy holder is dead, as in has been for some time, and the money is still coming to the firm from the account?"

Taylor heard Ronnie draw in a deep breath. Taylor closed her eyes and waited for the blast—telling her that she was jumping to conclusions and that she needed to stop looking for problems when there were none. But Ronnie didn't do that.

"Taylor, you need to bring me what you have. The company you're working for is committing insurance fraud. And if you have anything to do with the accounts, including knowledge, when the Feds step in, you're going to jail with them. How sure are you that this is going on, and how deep are they?"

"Deep, as up the creek without a paddle and the boat has a big hole in it. I don't want to go to prison. I have...I...I'm going to be sick. You have to...can you tell me where I can go to get rid of this stuff?"

"I'm sending Devin for you right now. And don't you dare argue with me. Bring everything you have right now."

"No, I can't. They...your family won't like that I'm bringing this to you too. Let me have the name of someone you think will help me and I'll go there now. Please?"

"You've already involved me, Taylor. If you don't let me help you, I'm going to prison too. Where are you? Neither Devin nor I will tell a soul where you are or that we talked to you."

"I'm at the Y on Tenth."

Devin didn't say much when he helped her into his SUV some thirty minutes later. He simply put her backpack into the trunk and drove them to the hospital. Taylor felt as if she was going to her execution and Devin and his wife were the executioners.

Chapter Eight

Byron watched the room before him. The people playing were enjoying themselves, yet he couldn't bring himself to join them. Several women, all Subs, were fucking each other and a man lying on the bed beneath them. He had one female spread across his face as he feasted on her pussy, another on his cock pumping up and down while she suckled on the pussy of a woman straddled over the man's chest in front of her. There was a fourth woman who was on her knees to his right finger fucking herself as she went back and forth between the two women at his cock. It should have been something Byron would have joined in on. His cock ached and he was hard as stone, but all he could think about was the woman back home.

"If you're thinking of getting out of the game, I'll buy all your clubs at whatever the asking price is." Byron looked at the man standing to his left, both shocked and intrigued by his generous offer. Marc Davidoff was a very good friend he had met in college.

When they had graduated, Marc moved back to Paris to be with his family to work in the vineyard. They had kept in touch over the years and whenever either of them was close enough to visit, they made sure that the club was open to them as well. Marc had been the one to introduce Byron to the Dom/Sub world.

"No, not selling. Though if I do, I'll let you know. I have something else on my mind tonight."

"Well, since I know it's not your lack of sales—congratulations on that, by the way—it must be your family or a woman. You're not bitching about your brothers like you normally do, even though I've asked several times tonight, so that leaves the woman. Who is she?"

Was it a woman? Byron didn't know, but one certainly was on his mind a great deal the last two weeks, especially today. The thought of Taylor coming to one of his clubs and wanting to play with him had his mind wandering at the oddest times.

"Her name is Taylor. She was injured a few weeks ago in another club. Her taste in hard core is rough and I think she got in over her head. She was bit, and bad enough that she had to be hospitalized when it got infected. Damon said it was probably from a tooth infection. She's incredibly beautiful, and I want her bad enough that others are just not good enough. She's a good friend of my brother, Jamie. And she lives with him."

"Jesus, man! You don't just have a problem. You have a bomb ready to detonate. You're brother's girlfriend is a Sub that you want to fuck that is into harder core than you are. Maybe you should just stay here; it'll probably be safer for you." Marc laughed.

"Jamie said she's just his friend, that there is nothing between them other than that. I believe him. As for harder core than me, I think not, my friend. I can still show her a thing or two about pain and pleasure."

Byron went back to his hotel room soon after that. His friend teased him a bit more, but their friendship was strong enough to take it. Besides, he wanted to go back to his computer and read what Bobby, his manager of "Tightly Bound," had said about Taylor.

Taylor had requested an invitation to check out the club and Bobby wanted to know how he should proceed. Byron wanted her to wait until he was home, which was still another week away, and told Bobby to do a complete background check, as usual. And to send her to the clinic to have the blood work done. He was also to send her the options sheet and tell her to bring it back in with her on Saturday night at seven o'clock. Byron was to arrive on Friday morning and figured after jet-lag, he would be ready for some fun with her.

Byron was in the shower when he thought about how she had responded to his command at the event. She had even called him "master" without any prompting. His cock stiffened when he thought about her voice when she had said it, soft and submissive.

Fisting his cock, he thought about how it would feel to have her tied before him, down on her knees and her hands behind her back. He would demand that she lick him, only the tip, and watch her tongue lap at him. Moving his hand along his shaft, he closed his eyes and could almost see her there. Running his thumb over the tip, he imagined her lips wrapped around him, her wet, hot mouth sucking him. He felt his balls tighten up and he reached down and squeezed them with his free hand, causing just enough pain that he moaned harshly. He would fuck her mouth, holding her head tight as he touched the back of her throat with is cock. Then before he exploded, he would bend her over his bench and ram his cock hard into her over and over until he came.

His climax shot out of him; long streams of his cum hit the shower wall as he continued to jerk his cock as he imagined being buried deep into her pussy. When he was finished, he leaned against shower wall while his body became his own again and his heart began to calm down. Turning off the water, he smiled. Just six more days and this would be a reality, he thought.

~~~

"How many people have you found in the files that you know are deceased? I know you have more information than you told us, spill it. I can't help you without that," Devin asked.

It was nearing one in the morning and Devin had started out with short, clipped questions. Now, while they were not as clipped, they were no less demanding. Maybe it was too nice-sounding to be a demand, but they both knew that was what he was doing. He was a smart man, much smarter than she had given him credit for. Ronnie was sweeter at her demands, but no less effective.

"I never wanted to get either of you involved, you know. I just wanted to get some information so that I could figure this out on my own. I'm terrified and you're not helping. The sooner you back the fuck off me; I'll be able to think."

He smiled. Damned Grant men. Why did they have to be so friggin' sexy when they did that? She could see a bit of Jamie in Devin's smile and even a little of Byron there. She wasn't going to think of either man; she so didn't want to cry again.

"No, you didn't. But we are involved now. And tomorrow morning, I'm going to give you a contract dated for yesterday that says that we are now representing you. You need us. Now quit stalling and tell me the whole story." Glaring didn't faze him either, she realized.

"On Thanksgiving, I was inputting some checks when I realized I had put in the same amount several times. I did a 'find' on the sheet and found the same dollar amount more times than I thought was a coincidence. I pulled the account numbers of those deposits then pulled the corresponding files. That's when I saw that they were dead."

"How many times and the names on the files?" he asked without looking up. This was the tricky part, she thought; now she found out how much trouble she was in.

"I have...would you like to see them?" Ronnie and Devin exchanged looks and Taylor stood to leave. "I knew this was wrong. When the Freedoms told me to put the payments in the ledger, I should have just done it and kept my mouth shut. But, oh no, not Taylor Bennett. She had to just dig deeper until she uncovered more problems than her ass could cover. Which you would think would be an ample amount being as my —" Ronnie's laughter had her stop. Taylor wasn't even aware she had been speaking out loud.

~~~

"You work for the Freedom brothers? Well, that explains a lot. I don't suppose you have it in writing that they gave you permission to update the accounts, do you?" Ronnie asked with a smile.

"Yes. I seldom see them and they are always leaving...you still want to help me? I don't understand. I thought that once you found out that I was using my own computer and keeping copies, you'd just wash your hands of me."

"No, we'd never...wait; did you say you've been using your own computer? Do they know this too?" Devin said as he walked over to the bassinet with his daughter in it.

Taylor had little experience with kids. She had been an only child and when her parents were killed when she was seven, she had gone to live with her maiden aunt. Taylor had never even held a kid.

"Well, sure. When the one they gave me died, I emailed them to let them know and asked them until I got a replacement, would it be all right if I used mine? Jason Freedom said yes and then I heard from Paul a few days later saying it was okay with him too. But that was four months ago and I've still not seen a replacement. So every day, I drag mine on the bus to work and then home again." He was smiling. Not a good one either, but one that made her think of a beast just realizing his prey was within his grasp.

"Taylor, I think I could fall in love with you. You have those emails, don't you?" She nodded. "Good girl, let's see what you have."

The head nurse came in at three to run her off. She packed up her things to leave immediately. Ronnie had been asleep since Taylor had pulled out her laptop. Devin was scribbling notes and looking over the copies of the files she had made the first day. She was nearly to the door when she realized he was right behind her.

"Come on, I'll take you home. It's too late for you to be out on the streets alone. If anything happened to you, Ronnie would kill me."

"No, that's all right, I can just take a bus. There's a hotel just down on Hudson that is cheap. Besides, I need to stop by the bank on the way in tomorrow—well, today—to give you those other drives. You go back to your kid and wife."

"Car, Taylor. And I'm not taking you to a hotel. I picked you up at the Y and that's where I'll take you back."

"The Y locks up at eleven. Seriously, I'll be fine. I've been doing this for some time. Go back upstairs and...shit, what the hell?" He grabbed her elbow and led her to his car before she could protest anymore.

"Why can't you just do what you're told? Damn it all to hell, woman! Do you have any idea what these men could do to you if they found out what you've been up to? Do you think that with this sort of money involved that they wouldn't take you out in a heartbeat to keep you from reporting them?"

"Let go of my arm." When he released her, she turned back to the street, but didn't move. "And what makes you think I give a shit?" She walked away then, toward the open street, and didn't look back.

Taylor didn't know how long she walked before exhaustion took her to the donut shop. She hurt, her leg was getting better, but she knew she had over done it tonight. She ordered a large cola and a cruller that she didn't want. Sitting in the booth, she stared out the window without seeing anything.

Christmas was in two weeks and she didn't know what to do with the gift she had for Jamie. Devin and Ronnie were now her lawyers and Damon was her doctor. Caitlynne Grant was the investigating officer on her bite mark and she had no idea what to make of Byron. Tears went unnoticed down her cheeks before she pulled out a notepad and began making lists.

The first thing she did was make a list of what she owed. It wasn't much. Rent at the Y was less than fifty bucks a week and there were no utilities. She did have to go to the Laundromat, but the only thing she really needed to wash right now was her under things and she thought she could wash those in the bathroom. She didn't have to buy food, not that it would do her any good. There was no kitchen she could cook it in and she didn't know how anyway. And she didn't have a cell phone, not that she didn't need one; she just couldn't afford it—especially now. That left her personal items. She was okay on tampons and shampoo, but she did need to get deodorant and toothpaste. The car was her biggest thing.

The guy at the shop had told her it would be over seven hundred dollars to fix it; he said that the book value was less than that. He told her if she scrapped it out, she might get around five hundred for it. Putting that into her credit list, she put down three hundred just to be on the safe side then found the card he had given her to call. With the cash she had now, not more than five hundred, she thought, that would still give her less than a grand. She thought about selling her computer and ditched that idea. She figured she wouldn't get much and, besides, it was all she had in the world right now. Taylor reached into her pack, pulled out the jewelers box nestled at the bottom, and opened it.

She had put this on layaway in June for Jamie for Christmas and made payments every week until she paid it off last week. It was a pair of diamond cuff links with his initials on them. He told her once when he became head of his department that's what he wanted. She had been determined to give them to him no matter what, even going without a few times when the Freedoms forgot to give her a check. She had paid nearly three grand for them even after the discount the owner had given her because she was his daughter's friend. She wanted him to still have them, but wasn't sure what he would do if she gave them to him. Closing the box, she put it back in the pack.

Taylor knew that a one-way plane ticket to Florida would be around a hundred and eighty dollars and then she would need to set herself up once she got there. She had emailed Josh and asked him if she came back, would he hire her as a waitress again? She hadn't heard from him yet. She pulled out her computer and using the network in the shop, checked her email for messages.

There was still nothing from Josh, but she did have one from Devin. He told her not to get the drives out today and to sit tight until he contacted her. He told her that she should receive a package sometime this morning at the law firm and to call him when she got it. He gave her both his home and office numbers, as well as his cell phone. He told her if anything came up between now and then she was to get to his office or call the police. She didn't have a clue what he thought would happen, but filed the information away for later.

The last email was from "Tightly Bound." They sent her the form to fill out telling them what she was interested in, how much pain she could deal with, and the toys she wanted used. It was a standard form, but this one had a place for comments. Taylor wasn't sure what sort of comments they expected her to make as she had never been there, but figured she would print the form up at work and fill it out on her lunch break. She was also to go to the clinic for a urine and blood test. Again, this was standard procedure.

By the time she was finished, it was nearly time for her to get into her room. She walked the eight blocks to the Y, thinking it was as good a time as any to begin her regimen of trying to save money. Later that same morning, she was walking in the door at just before nine when the courier showed up with the package.

Chapter Nine

Byron's plane landed at two in the afternoon on Friday. He had had a great exhibit and sales and felt really good about life in general. He was looking forward to sleeping in his own bed and in his own time zone. The last few pieces of his art that hadn't sold, three of the thirty that he had sent over were going to be on display in the gallery that the show had been held in, so he didn't even have to make arrangements to have them shipped back. When he exited the plane, Byron was surprised to see Spencer there waiting for him.

"I thought we could have a late lunch. O'Malley is taking Meggie shopping for gifts and I thought you and I could talk about what we're getting Mom again." Byron smiled at his brother.

Spencer had remarried this past summer. His wife, Caitlynne O'Malley Grant, was a detective for the local police department. And even though her last name was now Grant, he still called her by her maiden name and she called him Grant. They had a very strange and loving relationship.

They ended up at one of their favorite places, the Cheesecake Factory in the Easton center, and after ordering a beer for Byron and a cola for Spencer, Byron sat back in his chair.

"Okay, what's going on? I know it's not Mom's gift. We both know that Devin already purchased the tickets for their cruise. It can't be because your wife isn't at home; she would probably welcome you with her. What has you so worked up that you'd cut class to pick me up in the middle of a school day?"

"What makes you think I don't want to be...ah fuck it. It's Jamie. I can't figure out what's up his ass. He snaps and snips at everyone. Even the dean has fallen victim to his less than charming attitude. And Mom said that if he doesn't show up this Sunday for dinner, she is going to be really mad. I think she's hurt that he won't talk to her about it."

"Have you tried talking to him? You and he seem to be the closest. I did try and call him while I was gone and he practically hung up on me. You're the one who told me that Jamie told Mom that he wasn't responsible for Taylor. Do you have any idea what he meant by that?" Byron thought that he knew what his brother's problem was, but didn't want to voice that just yet.

"I'm not sure she's living there anymore. I don't know everything, but when I went there a few days after she checked herself out of the hospital, he told me that she moved out. When I pressed, he snarled at me. I think it has to do with Taylor, though I'm not sure how. I wanted to ask you. You seemed to...I mean, you were able to get through to her faster than anyone that night and she...well, I couldn't help but notice she called you 'master.'"

Byron had anticipated this question coming up. He had been thinking about how to handle the question and thought that the best way was the smartest. Give as much information as he could without giving away anything—worked for him.

"If you're asking if I've slept with her, no I haven't. I do have some experience with some of the BDSM crowd and from the wounds I saw on her earlier that day, I just guessed that was the best way to handle her. She's a submissive and sometimes just putting the right tone in your voice has her doing just what you want." Byron could tell that Spencer wasn't satisfied with the half answer, but he didn't press.

"I probably don't want to ask this, but well, you didn't say you weren't going to sleep with Taylor, but that you haven't—as if to say it's not out of the question. Could that be what Jamie is all upset about?"

"Jamie and Taylor aren't having sex. If he had been then he would have seen what I did the day I went by his house. She was whipped and the marks were fresh—unless he put them there, which I doubt. And I wasn't there to put the moves on her. She had hung up on me earlier and I was there to take my pound of flesh.

She came out of the bathroom with a towel around her and I saw the marks. Nothing happened."

Their dinner came and the waitress brought them refills. Spencer took a call from his wife and Byr looked over the room. He wanted to get back to his house and rest up and he wanted to see what sort of information Bobby had gotten back from the clinic regarding Taylor. He didn't want to try and smooth ruffled feathers between his families. He knew he would be spending the evening with some or all of them, but he just wanted to get home.

"O'Malley said to tell you we are having a late dinner at our house. Devin and Ronnie are bringing the baby over and we are to give suitable oohs and ahhhhs over her and shower her with gifts. Did you get her something in France?"

He had, actually, a gift for everyone. But he had gone a little overboard on the gifts for the new baby. He loved having nieces and nephews; it made him smile to think of the way they acted like their fathers. He thought about his brother having a daughter and smiled. He wondered how protective Devin would be of the girl when she got old enough to date someday.

~~~

Taylor went to "Tightly Bound" at four-thirty. She stood outside the doors and debated about going in. Her invitation was for tomorrow night and wondered if they would just let her sit in the open room and watch. She went to the door several times before someone coming out held it open for her to go in, taking the choice from her.

The woman at the front told her to wait after she had asked to see Taylor's ID. Lynn, her name tag had said, was on the phone and smiled at Taylor several times as she listened to whoever was on the other end. This was stupid, Taylor thought. She needed to go home and get her crap out of the car so that the junk dealer could pick it up tomorrow. While she was debating the sanity of coming here, her stupid cell phone went off. It was Devin again, of course.

The package that Devin had sent over was the cell phone currently in her pocket. He had put a note inside the box telling her who was programmed into it and the corresponding number to push to reach them. The stupid thing was even fully charged. She called him from the office phone when she called to tell him she had gotten it.

"Is there something wrong with the phone? The guy at the kiosk said it was top of the line. It even has Internet service."

"No, not that I know of. You said to call you when it got here and I'm doing that. If you wanted me to call you with it, then you should have said to do that. Hang on." She hung upon him. Smiling, she called him back. She could hear him sputtering about being hung up on when he answered.

"It wasn't necessary for you to hang up on me, Taylor. I could have waited until you had to call me again." She didn't tell him she had no intentions of calling him unless there was no other recourse. But she kept that little bit of information to herself. "I'll be sending you emails over the next several days and I want you to stop making copies of things. I don't want you to get caught nor for the Freedoms to have any reason to mistrust you. All right?"

Taylor had already decided to stop making copies, but again, kept that thought to herself. She debated all day as to whether or not she should tell him of her plans and had decided she wouldn't. It wasn't as if they were close, so what did it matter that she was going back home as soon as Christmas was over whether this was finished or not?

"You know, I haven't talked to the Freedoms in a month as much as I've had to talk to you today. Don't you have a kid or something you can be with? I have a life and it's hard to enjoy it if you're constantly calling me," she told him in way of answering.

"I've just got off the phone with the FBI. They'll want to speak to you in the morning and they want to know if eight o'clock is all right. You can meet with them at my office if you feel more comfortable that way. I'll be there, of course."

Her throat closed up and the room started to roar around her. Swaying, she reached blindly for something to hold onto when she touched the man behind her. Clutching his sleeve, she didn't even look around, but held on tightly. He guided her through the doors and suddenly, she was on a sofa with her head between her knees. She could hear Devin and his shouts from the phone, but she still couldn't get past the word FBI.

70

"Here, drink this," the man said as he shoved a small glass of something into her hand. She didn't even look or ask, but threw the contents to the back of her throat all at once. Her face felt as if she had lit a torch to it and her throat felt like someone had taken a sandblaster to it. Coughing hard and trying to catch her breath, she looked at the man on the floor in front of her. He nodded to the cell phone while he smiled at her.

"Damn it all to hell and back, something's happened to her. I haven't a clue...Taylor!" She had put the phone to her ear and jerked it back when he shouted her name.

"Christ, I'm right here. I had a...moment. I don't want to talk to the...I don't want to talk to them. Why the hell are they involved anyway? You said that you'd make sure that I was covered."

"This is a serious case of insurance fraud. Are you alone? Damn it, this is not a conversation that we should be having where people can hear us." She looked at the phone in her hand and nodded once then put it back to her ear.

"You're absolutely right. Good-bye." And she turned off the phone after she closed it. She didn't call him; he called her. Taylor was getting sick of his bossiness anyway.

"I'm sorry, I didn't catch your name." The man grinned again. She wasn't sure, but she felt like he was sizing her up for some reason.

"Bobby. We weren't expecting you until tomorrow night. The owner said to tell you to wait here and he'll be more than glad to come in and talk to you."

"I've changed my mind. I think I'll just come back tomorrow night. Maybe. I don't know. I just...what's so funny?" She found herself wanting to smack him. His knowing grin had her feeling like she was in trouble and he was going to enjoy watching her get her punishment. Seeing that they were in a bondage club, she thought he wasn't far off the mark.

"Nothing. You are gorgeous, aren't you? The boss said for you to wait. I don't think he'll be too happy with us if you leave."

Taylor stood up. She would leave when she wanted to, not when some boss decided she could. Bobby stood too — close.

"I want to leave. I don't want to have to hurt you, but I will if you don't back off. I've had a really shitty day and I wouldn't mind

71

in the least to take it out on you. You can tell your boss whatever you want. If he wants to revoke my invitation because I didn't wait, then I guess that'll be fine too. I'll be leaving the area soon, so what do I care what he does?"

"He should be here soon and you can tell him yourself. I think it would be in your best interest to wait for him." Taylor didn't like where this was going. She had the feeling that she didn't want a meet and greet with the owner.

She pushed the man away from her and he crashed over the little table behind him. He was moving to get up when she turned on her heel and left the office. She was out the front door and into the street before the man could catch her. She was darting down a side street when she thought she saw Byron coming toward her.

Chapter Ten

When Bobby had called Byron out of a deep sleep, his first instinct was to rip the man wide open. Then he realized what he was saying. Taylor was there.

"Keep her there. I don't care if you have to tie her to something to do so, you keep her there." He was pulling on his jeans as he barked the order.

"Lynn said she's been outside for a good ten minutes talking to herself and it looked like she was debating on whether or not to come in. Lynn said that she finally sent Joey out to ask her what she was doing when she came in on her own. Lynn called me as soon as she realized who she was. Shit! Gotta go, boss. Hurry, she looks ready to pass out."

Of course, that didn't help. Byron now had the added worry that something else had happened to her and he would have to take her back to the hospital. If she went back to that club and got hurt again, he was going to paddle her but good. And, of course, that set off a whole new set of images of things he was going to do to the delectable Ms. Bennett.

When he got to the club, he was ready to roar out his disappointment. She was gone and not only that, but she had thrown Bobby to the floor to escape. He didn't know whether to laugh or cry. Bobby was so impressed with Taylor all he could do was go on about how Byron had maybe misjudged her and she, too, was a Dom. Lynn was putting an ice pack on Bobby's head while Byron tried to figure out if this would make her not want to come in tomorrow night. He didn't know if he would be able to make it if he didn't get to play with Taylor. His cock was at a raging hard-on state now and he thought he would explode if he didn't get to bury himself inside of her soon.

Byron didn't know why this woman, of all the women he knew, made him feel like this. Since the first time he had seen her, all pink and rosy from the shower with that big towel almost not wrapped around her, he had wanted her. The sight of her beautiful globes of muscled flesh with marks on them made him want to drop before her and nip at them. He wanted to drag her across his lap or tie her to his bench and turn her ass red with his hand until she screamed out his name. The thought of tasting her, all of her, made his mouth dry. The need to bury himself deep within her made his cock ache so much that no amount of relieving the pressure in the shower helped now. He was having the worst case of lust he had ever had for a woman and didn't have the slightest idea why.

"Sorry, boss. But she was determined to leave. I'm not sure what I could have done short of hitting her over the head to keep her here. She's a little scary." He didn't tell Bobby that he had probably come on too strong. The man felt bad enough for not helping him out.

"Don't worry about it, Bobby. But do me a favor, email her and tell her that we're sorry about tonight and if she comes tomorrow night, we'll give her a month of membership for free. Hell, tell her we'll be glad to give her six months if she comes back."

"I'll do that, boss, but I don't think she'll take the membership. She mentioned that she was leaving the area soon and that she didn't care if you revoked her invitation or not. She told Lynn that she just wanted to sit in the open area and watch. Then that phone call came in and she looked ready to pass out. If I hadn't have come up behind her when I did, I'm sure she would have fallen on her pretty face."

"Leaving? Did she say when or where she was going? Damn it. If she thinks that she's getting away from me that easily, then she'll have to think again." He chose to ignore Bobby thinking Taylor was pretty. He didn't know why that should have bothered him so much, but it did.

Byron went to his brother's house, but not before stopping at his apartment in town. He gathered up all the gifts, his camera, and anything else he could think of to take over with him. He was short tempered about Taylor and he was tired. He probably should stay home, but when there was a family get together, then that meant family — all of them.

Jamie, of course, was the last to arrive. He came in the door with a chip on his shoulder and anyone within two feet of him could tell. When he snarled at Byron, all hell broke loose.

Byron drew back and hit his brother in the face. He had been aiming for his nose, but Jamie had turned and Byron hit his eye. Jamie was luckier in that he hit Byron on the nose and blood erupted, splattering down both men and onto the floor. Fists swinging and bodies being thrown the floor ensued. And when a sudden missile zoomed past Jamie's head and shattered against the wall just behind them, they both froze in motion and looked at the woman holding another glass in her hand.

"You damned near hit me!" Jamie still hadn't released Byron's throat and Byron still had an ample hand full of the Jamie's hair clutched in his fist.

"Well, I guess my aim is off. Shall I try again?" Cait tossed the glass up in the air and catching it, drew back to throw when Spencer came up and took it from her. She turned and smiled at her husband and both Byron and Jamie relaxed. It was short lived. She turned back to them so quickly that they staggered back. "Office! Now!"

She turned and walked toward the office without turning to see if either man followed. Byron looked at Jamie and then let him go. He was halfway to Cait when Jamie snarled again.

"I will not be told to go to the office like I'm some sort of child. I'm not five years old. I'm out of here." When he turned to leave, heading for the door, Spencer, Devin, Damon and Nicky blocked his path. They walked him backwards toward the study door.

When the three of them — Byron, Jamie and Cait — were inside, she turned and locked the door. She walked to the front of the desk, pointed to the two chairs facing it, and waited.

Byron hated being treated this way too. But he was also a little afraid of his sister-in-law. Especially now. A hormonal pregnant woman who carried a gun and knew how to inflict pain was no one he wanted to fuck with. So with that in mind, he went to the chair and sat.

"James Grant, I'm having a really shitty day. You've ruined my welcome home party for my brand new niece, you've bled on my carpet, and I had to break a perfectly good glass to make you two stop before you hit one of the children running around here. I would suggest that you get your ass over here and sit down right now."

"Fine. But I'm not talking. This is ridiculous; he started it. Everyone keeps asking me where Taylor is, is Taylor all right? Have you talked to her lately? She isn't my responsibility. It's not like I bit her. She's the one who got herself into this mess in the first place. How the hell was I supposed to know she was a pervert?" He flopped into the other chair and Byron heard it groan.

"I didn't start anything. I didn't even ask you about her. I asked you if you liked your new office, you son of a bitch. Then you got all defensive. I guess I didn't realize you were so sensitive. As for Taylor, you moron, she is not a pervert. I'll beat the shit out of you again if you so much as think it." When both of the men stood and started to lunge at each other, Cait simply cleared her throat. When they looked at her this time, she was holding her gun in her hand.

"Are you going to make me shoot one of you in the leg? I've had about enough of this shit. Sit down and shut up!" She set the gun on the desk behind her when they both sat back down. "My head hurts, Spencer took away my chocolate milk, and you two are acting like tyrants. I'm going to ask you about Taylor. And before you get all high and mighty with me, it's because I might need her for something in the future."

"For the hundredth time! I. Am. Not. Her. Keeper," Jamie said.

"No, but at one time, you were her friend. That is until she needed you. But like you've said, it's none of your business. I just...I talked her in the hospital that day. I'm assuming now it was after you threw her out of your house. She looked broken and defeated. I...you called her a pervert. Why?"

"She lets men beat her? She gets off on pain? What kind of person...she isn't anything like I thought she was. A sexual deviant is what she is. I want nothing to do with her, and to be honest, I can't believe you'd let her be around Meggie. What if she tries something on her?"

Cait's hand was out and across his face so quickly that Byron nearly tipped the chair back. He didn't know which of them had a more surprised look on their face. But Cait's was certainly more angry.

"How dare you accuse me of being an unfit mother. Do you think Taylor wanted to be raped like that? Do you think she had any inkling that he was going to do the things he did to her?"

"Raped? No, she wasn't raped. She lied to you. She...why does he get to leave?" Byron had had enough of Jamie calling Taylor names and if he didn't leave soon, blood was going to be shed again. Only this time, it wouldn't be his.

He was nearly to the door when he turned to Jamie. "You've made your opinion of me pretty clear, Jamie. I'm a sexual deviant; I'm not fit to be around my niece and probably the others as well. I'll not subject you to myself any longer."

"What are you talking about? We were talking about Taylor. And there isn't any way she can claim rape when that's what she wanted. I've read enough to know those sort of people—"

"I'm those sort of people, you judgmental asshole. I'm a Dom and not only that, but I own several clubs that specialize in that sort of people's deviance. Let me ask you something, Jamie, have you ever held a woman still when you made love to her? Have you ever spanked a woman during sex?"

"That's not the same thing. It was playing around. Taylor purposely went there to be—"

"It's exactly the same thing. Only in order for us 'sexual deviants,' as you called us, to really enjoy it, I need to dominate. I need to exert power over the woman I have sex with. Do they enjoy it? Hell yeah they do. Having a woman bow before me, take me into her mouth while tied down is a big turn on for me. And for Taylor, she wants someone to tell her when she can come, when she can touch or be touched. I haven't the slightest clue how she was raped, but I intend to find out and...talk to the bastard."

"It was her list, the one she filled out before they let her come inside. He didn't...she didn't want him to beat her and he did. As for the bites, that was him too. He hurt her. And I'm running an investigation into maybe him hurting others as well, men and women." Byron completely forgot about Cait in the room and flushed with heated embarrassment. She shrugged when he looked at her.

"Why didn't she use her safe word? If he was doing something he wasn't supposed to, she should have used her safe word and he would have stopped." Byron had had it wrong. Taylor wasn't hard core, she was a victim. And not only a victim, but she had been mistreated by her friends because of it. He wanted to find her, find her soon.

"She did. She shouted it out to the room the first time he hit her with the whip, then the fourth time and the fifth. He continued over and over until she fainted from pain, she told me. He bit her, several times I might add, after she was unconscious. I was able to get a name from the owner, though he wasn't really happy about it. According to the video of the incident, she said her safe word eighteen times before it was all finished."

"I...he bit her while she was...that's sick. How could she let...I guess she didn't let anyone do anything, did she?" Jamie asked no one in particular.

"No, her rights were taken from her the moment she said her word the first time, and every time after that. They didn't even call an ambulance for her, but put smelling salts under her nose until she woke then sent her out the door. The owner tried to tell one of my men that she was drunk or on drugs, but that didn't pan out. She'd had a blood test a few days before and she tested clean. Since I've started this investigation, there have been quite a few others come forward. All of them with the same wounds."

Jamie got up. When he started toward Byron, he stiffened, ready for another fight with him. They stood staring at each other for several seconds until Jamie turned back to Cait.

"You're a good person, Cait. Thanks. I still don't...I'm not sure how I feel about this, but I'm sorry. Very sorry that I brought it here, to your house." Jamie turned back to Byron. "Are you seeing Taylor?"

"Not yet. I'd like to, and I'm actually working on it. Is that all right with you?" Byron realized that it mattered to him that Jamie was all right with it too.

"Yes. I think so anyway. I'm still not...I don't know what I feel about this or her. I don't even know why I'm so mad at her yet. But if you hurt her, hurt her like I did, or that bastard did, I'll kill you. Understand me?"

"Yes. Jamie, if you want to come down to the club some night...I can —" Byron started.

"I'm so not ready for that, but thanks. Maybe later. Right now...I'm sorry Cait, but right now, I'm going home. I've...it's too much and I need to get my head on straight. Byr, I'm sorry for this. But I'd really like to know when you find the bastard. I really want to ask him a few questions of my own." Jamie opened his arms and Byron stepped into his embrace. He didn't realize how much he needed his brother until then.

After he left, Byron sat back down with Cait. "Tell me everything you have, please. If he did that to her, she's going to need...I'm seeing her tomorrow night at the club. I'll need to know what I have to deal with to help her."

~~~

"It's the best I can give you, little girl. I wish I could help you out, but it just ain't a whole lot of demand for a thirty-year-old car, even if it is just for parts."

Taylor had been haggling with the scrap dealer for over an hour. He would only give her two hundred for the piece of crap car. She supposed that was better than the one hundred he had first offered her. Sighing, she nodded and took the cash. She would just have to figure out how to get the rest of the money for her ticket.

So far, her list of things to do was getting longer, not shorter. Pulling it out, she crossed out "selling car" and then looked her list over. Of the dozen or so things on the list, she had only crossed out two — the car and going to the club. She wasn't going there.

The man had tried to keep her there and that frightened her more than she wanted to admit. All she could think about was the other club and waking up hurting and in a strange place. Thankfully, she was healed, but she was still terrified of someone taking advantage of her again. When the cell phone rang again, she decided to answer it. Devin had called her over a hundred times since yesterday afternoon, she was sure of it.

"What?" Okay, she probably could have been a lot more polite, but she didn't ask him for the phone nor for him to keep calling her on it.

"I'm going to try my best to be nice to you. Ronnie said that I may have been a little harsh in my telling you about the FBI." Taylor smiled. She would just bet that's not all Ronnie had said.

"You think? I don't know, telling me one minute that you are going to have my back and that you'll help me then telling me that you've just talked with the Feds...nope, harsh is an understatement. I'm not talking to anyone. I've decided that I don't want to pursue this thing anymore. On Monday, I'll go by the bank, give you the thumb drives, and let you deal with it. I'm finished."

"It doesn't work that way, Taylor. You're up to your pretty ass involved now. Once you make it known that you have knowledge, you need to stick with it. I'm sorry. The Feds still want to meet with you this weekend. When can you come by my office? I'll meet you there anytime you want."

She looked across the street at the pretty lights in the shop window and felt the tears roll down her cheeks. Why, why did she ever think that doing the right thing would actually be the right thing to do? Now she was in trouble. Again.

"Taylor? Are you still there? I do want to help you. I'm sorry that—"

"Yeah, so am I. I'll call you later, Mr. Grant. I'm kind of in the middle of something here." She closed the phone and sat down on the bench outside the garage where her car had been.

Every time she thought she was getting ahead, something always hit her broadside and her nicely laid plans crumbled. All she had wanted to do was to start over, come to Ohio, get a good job, a nice apartment, and a guy to call her own. And what did she end up with? No car, no apartment, and not an even a mediocre job. She pulled the list out of her pocket again.

She couldn't even mark through three more things on the list now. She wasn't going to go to the bank and give the drives up, she wasn't going to get to quit her job, nor was she going to ignore any contact with the Feds. Wadding up the list, she started to throw it in the trash can and then started to smooth it out. Fuck them, she thought and stuck it back into her pocket.

She went back to the Y and dug out something to wear. She was going to that club, but she wasn't going there to play. She just needed to be around people like her. Someone who wouldn't be repulsed by what she was. She felt that way about herself enough. Picking up a bag of apples and a bottle of water, she felt better than she had in days.

Chapter Eleven

Byron had been at the club since noon. He had tried working at home but couldn't seem to concentrate on anything other than Taylor. He wasn't getting much more done here, but at least he could pretend more with the computer up in front of him.

Rape. He had heard that "The Flogger" had a semi bad reputation, but he'd really never put much thought into it. He had figured that if they were that horrible to their customers, then they would end up at his place. And he couldn't help but feel that he had let Taylor get hurt because of his greedy thoughts.

Looking at his watch for the thousandth time, he groaned. She wouldn't even be here for another three hours and he was about to burst with need to touch her. Smiling, he thought touching her was only part of what he wanted to do to the bossy Ms. Bennett.

He walked to his personal room and turned on the lights. His room wasn't anything like the ones in the club. He had toys and equipment here that had been specially designed and built for him. Closing the door behind him, he walked to the wall unit and opened the doors. Every imaginable toy or device was here, some that he had designed himself. He pulled his newest toy off the hook. He had picked it up while he had been in France.

It was a flogger, but different than the others that he had. This one, while made of leather, the strips had been feathered along both edges so that it was as soft as a real feather. He couldn't wait to run it over Taylor's skin to watch her eyes glaze over with need. He would have her tied to his cross while he did it and not allow her to make a sound when he slapped it over her ass. He leaned against the wall and closed his eyes. If she didn't show tonight, he was going to be in serious trouble.

At five, he ate a light dinner and was nearly finished with it when Bobby came into the office. The look on his face would have been comical if it hadn't made Byron a little nervous.

"She's here, boss. Lynn said to tell you that she needs you up front, pronto. There is a little trouble."

Byron was out of the chair in a heartbeat and striding to the front of the club. He could hear the voices before he saw them. And when he did, he stopped and watched. He held Bobby back as well.

"You touch me again, you perverted dick, and I'll feed that small twig and berries of yours to you. I said that I wanted to be alone; alone as in you are nowhere near me. Got it?"

"You don't know what you're missing, honey. And I don't have any sticks with me and especially no fruit; I don't think they let you bring stuff like that in here. How 'bout you let my bud Pete here and me keep you company? We can have a real good time."

When the man stepped forward, so did Taylor. Byron was ready to leap to her defense, but her next move startled a laugh from him instead. She took both men out in one move.

The man called Pete had tried to grab her arm so Taylor rammed her forehead into his nose. It was a slick move, and quick. Pete hit the floor, out cold. The first guy had tried to move behind her and she simply turned and kneed him. He did get in a fast jab to her jaw before he, too, hit the floor. When she backed up quickly to avoid another patron's grab, Byron wrapped his arm around her waist and pulled her against him.

"Taylor, it's me, I've got you." He felt her relax for all of five seconds, and then she brought her heel down on his foot. He might have laughed if it hadn't hurt so much. He turned her around and tossed her over his shoulder and smacked her ass. Turning to Bobby, he told him to throw out the trash and take away their membership. Then he took the now cussing Taylor to his office.

"I'm going to put you down now. If you try to hurt me again, or leave, I'm going to beat your ass, do you understand me?" When she didn't answer, he swatted her on the ass again. If she didn't answer soon, he was going to come in his pants.

"Let me down, you overgrown ox. I don't know how you found me, but I want you to tell that brother of yours to fuck off and die." He swatted her again. He wasn't sure which of his brothers she was talking about, but it was as good a reason as any to get to spank her again.

"Are. You. Going. To. Behave? I'll not ask you again, Taylor. You will answer me or I'll tack another punishment onto the two you already have." He waited and just when he rose his hand to deliver another smack, she answered.

"Yes, I'll behave. I hate you. Now put me down." He smacked her again. Christ, if he kept this up, they would never make it to the room before he dropped her to the floor and fucked her right here.

"You'll answer me correctly. Do it now. You have three punishments coming; do you want to try for four?" He wanted her to go for five or six, but wasn't so sure who he was going to be punishing more, her or him.

"Yes, master. I'll behave." He slowly lowered her to her feet but didn't let her go. Grabbing both her hands and holding them behind her back, he pressed her closer to his body. He watched as her eyes widened at his erection pressing into her belly. Leaning down slowly, he brushed his mouth over hers.

Just that simple touch had him groan. She was soft and warm; her breath was sweet and slightly minty. He nipped at her lower lip and when she groaned, he ran his tongue along her lips. When she opened under his mouth, Byron let go of her hands and cupped her ass under her skirt. He couldn't feel anything but hot flesh. He knew in a small part of his mind that she was probably sore, but he needed to feel her wrapped around him. Want slammed into him, making him dizzy with need so desperately that he had to press her against the closest wall or fall to his knees with her. But that simply made him needier, especially when she wrapped her legs around his hips and locked her ankles.

"Baby, I want you, now. I want to fuck you so bad I hurt." He had never admitted to a Sub before how he felt. He gave the orders, he was in charge, but right now all he could think about was getting her naked and him inside of her. The chirping of a phone and the pounding at the door nearly made him whimper. Taylor did.

"What the fuck do you want?" he snarled to the door, and Taylor giggled. He turned to look back at her, still wrapped around him, and laughed. Christ, he wondered, how could either of them think this was funny?

"He probably wants to know why you're in his office. I would. I bet it's not every day that a customer breaks into his office to fuck someone against his walls." He didn't answer her, but let her slide down his body and held her. The knock at the door and her phone again made him need to step away. With a quick kiss, he walked to the door and stepped out.

"Boss, I was just wondering if you're out for the night? I know that you was waiting on her and all, but what should I tell anyone who asks?"

"Tell them that you don't know where I am and don't know when I'll be back. If it's my family and there's an emergency, then go to the intercom and page me. I'll hear it." At least he hoped he would. Right now, the buzzing in his head was making him dizzy. When he walked back into the office, he knew something had changed with Taylor.

"That was your brother, Devin. He's a tenacious bastard, isn't he? Anyway, I asked him if he sent you to follow me and he said that he wouldn't wish that on his worst enemy. He said that anyone who wanted to hurt me should take their chances, that I'm more than capable of taking care of myself. He's slightly pissed off at me right now."

"No, he didn't send me anywhere." He moved cautiously toward his desk. He was reasonably sure she would hurt him and very soon. Byron wasn't sure if he should smile or not, and when he looked at Taylor, he decided not.

"Then I started looking around. These pieces look like your art. I have two pieces that Jamie...your other brother gave me that look a lot like these." He heard the slight catch in her voice and wanted to pound Jamie all over again.

"Yes, they are. Taylor, this —"

"Don't! I've worked this out for myself; the very least you can do is let me tell you. I wondered why such a prestigious club would send me an invitation to visit. I mean, you had a waiting list of over six years when I asked several months ago. Then, suddenly,

I'm all in. I never gave it much thought at the time, but now I do. You own this club, or at the very least you run it."

"I own it. Let me…" He closed his mouth. She looked ready to boil over and he thought the best thing was…well, the best thing for him would be to let her calm a little.

"Own it, which means that you're responsible for me being here. And more than likely for the generous offer of six months of free membership because of what happened the…he knew you were coming, that young man at the door, he told me the boss—I'm assuming he meant you, wanted to speak to me. Damn, you've been playing me all along. What an idiot! I just keep digging myself in deeper and deeper, don't I?"

She paced back and forth in front of the desk. Byron watched her, wanted her. Her temper made her more beautiful and he wondered, not for the first time, how she would look when she came. When he realized that she had stopped moving, he looked up at her face. Shit!

"I'm not going to lie to you. I want you, Taylor. I want to see you bound and at my mercy. I want to play with you in the worst way." She stared at him then looked around the room again. He couldn't tell what she was thinking, and when she spoke, he nearly swallowed his tongue.

"I'll play with you. I'll play tonight, but never again. I want you to stay away from me, and your family to stay away as well. Deal?"

"I can't speak for my brothers. For as much as I want you, I can't make a promise to you that I can't back up. I'm sorry."

She sat in the chair across from his desk and looked at him. He could see the tears welling up in her eyes and he hurt because of them. He nearly got up and pulled her into his arms and that confused him more than his need for her. Byron had never wanted to comfort a woman, had never wanted to be near one when the waterworks started. But this woman made him want—no, made him need to hold her. He didn't want to think about what that meant, nor where it was leading.

"I just wanted to live my life like a normal person. I didn't want to be a sexual deviant. I didn't want to be perverted and ashamed of what I need. I just wanted a job, a career, and something...something else." Her voice was small and childlike even if the wording wasn't. His heart broke. He went to her, kneeled before her, and pulled her into his arms. She broke down and started sobbing.

"Taylor, honey, don't. You aren't either of those things. You're a beautiful, vibrant woman—sexy and not afraid to express yourself. Don't put yourself down, please?"

~~~

Taylor was going to take what she needed, even if it were for this one night with this one man. He made her feel things she had never felt with Josh or the man at "The Flogger." She felt safe and protected and she had never felt that before. Not sure she was doing the right thing, she stood up, took several steps back from him, dropped to her knees, and bowed before him.

It was several seconds before he moved. She was sure that he was going to tell her to go, to get out of his office, but he didn't. Byron stood up and over her.

"Are you ready to obey me? Be my slave, my submissive?" Her heart started beating faster at the tone of his voice. She could feel her pussy gush with need.

"Yes, master, I'm ready to be your slave for tonight." She told him the only way she knew how as his submissive that she would play, but only this once.

"You have three punishments coming. They are severe and you will have to pay those before I feel that you are sufficiently ready to be fucked. You understand that, slave?"

"Yes, master. I understand three punishments before you will fuck me." She had learned from Josh to repeat everything he said to her. That way, if she didn't understand or he wanted more or less than she was repeating, then he would be able to know without adding an extra punishment because she had misunderstood. "I'm ready to pay for my indiscretions."

"Good. And I know you understand how this works. I'm going to explain it again. When you say your word, everything, no matter what we are doing, will stop. You'll go home and nothing will be talked about. Then after thirty days, if you would like to return, we can try again. Understand? Now stand and come with me. You'll need a safe word."

"Daisies"

Chapter Twelve

Byron led her to his room and watched her. She never looked around, never even looked up from the floor. He knew what she was doing, waiting for him, for him to give her permission to look and to touch. He had hoped she would at least peek so that he could see her reaction. But he was also thrilled that she was such a good Sub. When she stood in the middle of the room, he smiled.

Her skirt was tiny, barely an inch below her pussy, and if she were to kneel down now, he was sure that he would see her ass. He suddenly wondered how much of her ass he had exposed when he had thrown her over his shoulder on the floor. Plenty, he would imagine. Her legs were bare and the "fuck me" boots she had on had four inch spiked heels. Her hair was pulled up into a braid that hung down her back in a thick plait. Her blouse, a see through white, was long sleeved and the cuffs hung over her hands. He had seen this trick before; it was so that the Dom couldn't see his Sub clench her or his fists. Her bra was dark and from what he could tell, very little of it—no straps, and her nipples were hard above the bit of lace. The only thing he couldn't see were her panties and he decided that was where he would start.

"Take off your panties, slave. And show me what you have beneath that skirt."

"I don't have panties on, master." His cock was nearly strangled in his pants and he swore he would wear a permanent scar from the zipper. He reached down and rubbed the abused flesh and nearly came. Christ, he needed to fuck her.

"Pull your skirt up over your waist and take off your shirt." She didn't turn to him, but did what he wanted; her ass was still

91

pink from when he had smacked her and he was suddenly glad she couldn't see him. He grabbed the wall for support.

Her blouse was next. He could still see the marks on her fair skin, bruised but faded. The wounds, scabs really, on her thighs were dark but healing. He wanted to go and find the man responsible and beat him within an inch of his life.

"Taylor, are you all right? Do you have any pain? I don't want to hurt you again." He did want to cause her pain, but pleasure too. He watched as she stiffened and her chin nearly rose before she remembered her promise.

"Yes, master. I'm fine. I have a slight pain in my thigh from his...from the deeper hurt, but I'm fine." Her voice was low and he could almost not hear her.

"Good. Come here and bow before me. I want you to remove my pants and suck my cock."

She turned then and slowly walked toward him. Her shaved pussy was the first thing he saw. Her boots, black and tight, molded to her calves like a second skin. The heels were sinking into the carpet and she had to walk a little slower than her normal gait. When she was a foot away, she dropped to her knees and put her hands on his belt buckle.

He had never had a submissive like her. She was perfect in every way. She never looked at him, only spoke when spoken to, and she obeyed without question. He was slightly disappointed in that. He wanted her to be bad, wanted to spank her for her misstep, but then the night was still young.

When his belt was off his pants and coiled neatly beside his foot, he watched as she unbuttoned the button and lowered the zipper. He could feel the slight discharge from his cock, the pre-cum staining his pants. When Taylor had his pants down around his ankles, he put his hand on her head as he lifted first one then the other foot so that she could slide them off. Next came his boxer briefs.

His cock strained against the material and he knew she could see how hard he was. When her small tongue came out and slid along her lips, he had to swallow a groan. She had never touched him, he realized. Even as she had pulled his briefs down, her fingers never grazed his skin. He was both excited and disappointed. When he held her head again to help her remove his briefs, he felt her warm breath on his thigh and tightened his grip on her hair. She was still holding onto his pants when she licked his cock, taking the stream of pre-cum into her mouth. When she closed her mouth over him and swirled her tongue over the head, he couldn't hold back the growl that rumbled from his throat.

"Touch me. Hold my cock and balls tight," he hissed at her. When her hand came up from the floor and wrapped around him, he pumped into her heat. Her other hand slid along his balls and grasped them tight, first one then the other. Her grip was tight, almost painful, and when she rolled his balls in her palm, he surged harder into her mouth and touched the back of her throat. Her moan moved along his shaft like a caress.

He could easily come right now. His balls were tight against his body and he could feel the tingle up his spine that told him just how close he really was. But he didn't want to come in her this way. He wanted to feel her pussy clasp around him and milk him. So with a great deal of effort, he pulled back from her mouth and hands.

"Stop. I want you to go over to the bench and receive your first punishment." She hesitated for several seconds and he couldn't blame her; need was racing over his skin like a living thing.

She walked over to the bench and waited for further instructions. She was standing there with just her skirt over her hips and her bra. The boots needed to stay, but the clothing had to go. He turned her around, unclasped the front closure of her bar, and let her breasts bounce free. There were magnificent.

Large and full, her breasts were as large as cantaloupes. Her nipples were nearly an inch long and as thick as his thumb. He wanted to see them clamped and he wanted to nibble on them, suckle them until she came. He moved to his cabinet and pulled out a drawer.

Byron had plenty of different types of rings, mostly cheap ones he only kept on hand to play, but he pulled out a pair of gold ones and brought them back to her. He pulled the first nipple into his mouth and he bit her, using his front teeth. He bit hard until she moaned

"So sweet, so delicious. I want to clamp these; I want to watch as they pink up and the blood rushes to them. I'm going to put those beautiful nipples in my clamps and make them ache for me." He stepped in front of her then and she could see the gold clamps in his hand. "Have you ever worn these before? Has anyone ever tightened these nipples in something like this before?"

"Yes. But I didn't like it. It wasn't what I wanted. It was too painful." He licked her left nipple and pulled the distended nipple into his mouth and bit it. She surged forward and tried to get him to take more. She didn't touch him, pull him to her, but she wanted to. He could see her clenched fists.

"I'm going to tighten these down until you tell me stop. If you don't like it, I'll remove them. I want them tender and ready for me, all right?" She nodded.

He had the first ring on her nipple before she realized it, he thought. He had been squeezing her breast so tight and sucking on just the tip that he was sure that she didn't notice that he had slipped it on. She looked down at it then up at him with a look of wonder on her lovely face. The dark gold against her skin looked good and he wanted her to touch it, but again, she didn't move her hands.

"Turn around and bend over the bench and put your hands near the cuffs. I'm going to strap you here then I'm going to punish you." He could hear his voice, the harsh sound of need.

The bench was about waist high. When a person was draped over it, as he wanted Taylor to be, he could fuck them as hard as he wanted. The legs were bolted to the floor and the hump itself was just firm enough to be supportive but also soft enough that it wouldn't hurt. He moved to the front of her when she leaned over it and strapped her hands to the leather cuffs on the floor. Moving to the side, he widened her legs and buckled them into the cuffs at each leg of the bench, leaving her feet a good three feet apart. Grasping her hair, he pulled her head up and pushed his cock to her lips with his free hand. She opened her mouth immediately and took him in. He fucked her mouth hard and when he felt himself get close again, he pulled back. His head was spinning like a top. When he stood behind her, he could see her pussy and how wet she was.

His cock hurt and seemed to jerk every time he looked from her ass and the tight rosebud there to the glistening lips of her pussy opened for him. He walked to his cabinet before he gave in and fucked her now.

"You've been a bad girl, slave, and you know what I have to do to bad slaves, don't you? I have to whip them. I'm going to whip you very hard." He reached out and rubbed his finger through her cream and brought it up over her crack. She was tight and he wondered if she had ever been fucked there, but didn't want to ask.

The first time the new flogger hit her flesh, she jerked. She whimpered slightly, but she didn't scream. Good, this was going to be much more enjoyable than he had imagined. He wanted to touch her pussy again, but knew that if he did, he wouldn't last much longer.

"You'll not come unless I tell you to, slave. And I don't want to hear another sound out of you. You make one noise and I'll double this punishment, understand?"

"Yes, master. I cannot come unless you give me permission and I'm not to make a sound or you'll double my punishment. I understand, master."

Byron ran the flogger along her ass and over and around each mound. He saw her jerk slightly, but she didn't make a sound. When he brought the flogger down again, and again, he watched as the skin reddened and puckered. Moving his finger through her cream again, he brought it to the small wounds with his fingers and rubbed the area he had just abused. When he was finished, he pushed his finger back into her heat and fucked her with his finger.

She was so tight that he barely got one finger in as far as his knuckle. As he pumped into her, he brought the flogger down three more times over her ass and watched as those brightened too. His hand was soaked with her juices and there was a small trickle of it going down her thigh. He wanted to lean down and lap her clean, suck her until she came and then maybe he'd stop. Sweat beaded on his forehead and he was nearly at his limit of endurance. He stopped her punishment long before he thought he should, but if he continued, he was going to fuck her or come all over her. He unbuckled her from the restraints and when she stood, he pulled her back against his front and rubbed her wrist.

Looking around the room, he tried to decide which of his toys to use next and which one would show the most amount of her body, especially her pussy and ass. He decided on the hanger that hung from the back of the room.

He had found this device in France as well. It looked just like a coat hanger in that it was in the same shape. It was attached to an adjustable chain link that could be lowered or raised, depending on the height of his playmate and if he wanted them to touch the floor or not. He wanted Taylor to touch.

Moving her in front of him, he could feel her pulse start to pick up when she realized where he was headed. Lifting her left arm, he put it into the cuff on one corner and then did the same to the right. He turned her around so that she was looking at him and pulled her in for a kiss.

He devoured her. Her mouth moved under his assault like it was hungry. He sucked her tongue into his mouth and nipped hard on it. She moaned into his mouth and he felt her move closer to him without touching. The rings on her nipples slipped deliciously over his skin and made him shudder. He wanted her to wrap her legs around his hips and impale her over his hard cock. But he knew as well as she did that waiting, though hard, was half the excitement.

Pulling away from her mouth and body, he went to the cabinet again. She could see him there now, and he moved to his left so that she could see what he had and how many toys he had collected. Her hiss of breath made him smile. She approved. But when he pulled out his whip, she moved back as far as she could and jerked on the hanger.

"I'm not going to hurt you. Stop pulling before you hurt yourself. Listen to me, Taylor; I'm not going to hurt you. I swear." He ran the long strips along her breasts and belly, never taking his eyes off of hers. "Feel the leather, the softness. I'm only going to tease you with it; I promise I won't hurt you with it." He continued to let the leather move over her skin, the thin strips wrapped gently over her clamped nipples. When he pulled the handle up and the leather moved over her shoulders, he reached down and took her hard nipple into his mouth.

All the while he ran the leather over her skin. When he moved to the other breast, he watched her face as he took the handle of his whip and moved it over her pussy. He knew that the clamps were making her nipples sensitive and needy. When he removed them, he was going to watch her face, see if she enjoyed them as much has he did having them there.

"You still have another punishment to go. I'm going to eat your pussy until I make you scream for release. But, slave, if you can go for thirty minutes of this punishment without screaming, I will give you a freebie, one to use anytime you want. Can you do that, slave? Can you not beg me for release for thirty minutes?"

Without waiting for an answer, he dropped to his knees and pulled her leg up over his shoulder. She was soaking wet, her juices were running down her thighs, and he licked them clean. He slowly made way up her thigh and using his fingers, opened her nether lips up.

Her clit was stone hard and swollen. Christ, she looked delicious, and he wanted to feast on her for hours. But he knew that he would be lucky if he made it the thirty minutes he had given her. His cock was hurting, and he didn't think he was going to last much longer. Using his tongue ring, he speared her opening and then closed his mouth over her clitoris. He wanted her to scream, wanted her to scream in the worst possible way.

~~~

She was never going to make it. There were no clocks in this room, but she knew without a doubt that it was going to be the longest half hour of her life.

His mouth closed over her clit and he began fucking her with his tongue. His strokes were hard and smooth, relentless and fast. The ball ring on his tongue was rubbing her clit hard then soft, slow then fast. She had never had a man touch her this way, lick at her with such intensity that she wanted it to last forever and to end quickly. She closed her eyes and tried to think of anything other than what he was doing to her body. When his hand came down hard on her ass, she opened her eyes and looked down her body at him.

"Watch me lick you. Watch me while I feast on this hot pussy of yours and think about my tongue lapping up your cream and drinking from you. Think about how much my tongue ring is fucking you and that soon, very soon, I'm going to be doing this with my cock. I'm going to fuck you hard, slave." His face was wet from her; his chin was glistening with her cream.

He moved his hand up her thigh as he watched her, and moved it to her ass. She knew what he was going to do, knew without a doubt that he was going to fuck her ass with his finger. When he pressed his finger against the tight ring, she nearly closed her eyes and threw back her head. No one had ever touched her there before. Josh said that it wasn't for him. She had always been disappointed about that, but was suddenly glad that he hadn't.

"Has anyone ever been inside you here, Taylor? Has anyone every fucked this tight ass of yours until you screamed?" His finger broke through the tight ring and she felt her eyes flutter again, but she never broke eye contact with him.

The pain was wonderfully dark. The more he moved his finger in and out of her, the better it felt. The burning was replaced with pleasure and, soon, it too was taking her closer to her orgasm.

"No. No one has ever...please, I-I please." She wasn't sure what she was begging for, but hoped that he knew. When he lowered his head to her pussy again, he moved his free hand to between her legs and pushed another finger into her tight channel.

She could almost feel them touching; his fingers were working her gently but firmly. Taylor moved her foot along his thigh and brushed over his erection and waited for him to tell her to stop. When he didn't, she pressed the toes of her booted foot over his cock and moved her boot up and down him, using just enough of the heel to make him shudder. He started pumping against her foot and she nearly screamed then. She would have if he hadn't inserted another finger into both of her virginal holes and pumped into her faster. She couldn't breathe, couldn't even remember how.

"Christ, you're killing me. I want to fuck this hot pussy of yours so bad that I can hardly think. Scream for me, baby. Scream for me so that I can end this and fuck you."

He nipped at her clit then, and then pulled it deep into his mouth and using his tongue, flicked at it relentlessly while he pumped his fingers into her deeper and harder. She was close, so close she had tunnel vision and saw stars flashing around the room. She opened her mouth to scream when she heard a beeping go off.

He pulled away. He didn't move from his knees but sat there on them and panted. Her own breath wasn't so steady, but she still needed to come. She wanted to come now. When he finally stood, she noticed that he didn't touch her, and when he reached up to unbuckle her wrist, he did so from behind her. Her swaying body brushed his once and his hiss nearly undid her.

"Go to the St. Andrews Cross and put your back against it. I want you to spread your arms and legs wide to the straps. You'll wait there for me until I return." Her legs were wobbly and weak and she staggered a couple of times on the way across the room. He walked with her, but he didn't touch her in any way. She could understand that. She was close enough to catch fire too.

When she backed against the St. Andrews, she spread her arms out. Her feet fit into the little grooves at the bottom and her heel of her boots slid off the back. She looked across from her and sucked in her breath.

Across from her was a mirror. Not a small one either. She would bet that it had been specially made as it was easily ten feet tall and the width of the wall—about fifteen feet. With her legs spread and her arms up over her head, she was open and wide. She could see everything. Her clit was red from his mouth and her thighs had tiny marks on them where he had nipped at her. Her nipples were a deep red and puckered so tight she wanted to touch them, run her fingers over them to feel the slight pain/pleasure that she knew would be there because of the clamps. The woman staring back at her looked dazed, wild, and ready to try or do anything.

"See what I see? See the way your body looks for me, ready and hot? I'm going to turn you around now then I'm going to tie you here and spank you. I'm going to watch your ass get redder and redder. Then I'm going to fuck you. Fuck you until we both can't walk."

He turned her around and then buckled her in the cuffs. She had been tied to this apparatus when the man at The Flogger had hurt her. Taylor could feel the panic begin to set in and she nearly said her safe word. Then Byron was in front of her again.

"I'm not going to hurt you. If you want to stop, now would be a good time to say your safe word and I'll take you home. I have to tell you Taylor, I'm so close that I fear disgracing myself at any minute." She laughed and knew that was what he had meant to happen. She nodded at him and he disappeared behind her.

The first lash was quick, nearly before she could settle in. He hit her across her ass and she pulled at the bonds. The next two were quick and then he took the soft flogger and tapped her pussy with it gently but firmly. Once, twice until she thought she would come from it. He brought the leather over her thighs next, then her shoulders twice before tapping it across her pussy again. Her body was on fire and knew that if he touched her there again, she was going to come.

Then his bare body slid over hers, his erection pressed hard against her ass, and she moaned. When he cupped her breasts and squeezed them, she didn't care if he beat her until she bled; she knew that she had to have him, have him deep inside her now.

"I'm going to fuck you now. I'm going to ram my cock deep into you and fuck you until you come hard all over me. Then I'm going to do it again." He voice whispered over her skin and she pressed back against him.

The first buckle fell from her wrist and she dropped her arm. She had been pulling against the restraints so hard that her arms were sore and tender. He ran his hand down her arm and pulled her hand to his ass. She grabbed it and shimmied against him. He felt so good, so hard. When the next buckle let go, he did the same thing, moved her hand to his ass and pushed his hard cock into the crack of her ass and fucked her this way. He had never buckled her feet, so when he turned her around and lifted, she wrapped her legs around him. At some point, he had taken off his shirt. His chest looked as though it had been sculpted from stone. There was no hair on his chest, but a small trail of it ran from his navel to his groin. His cock was strained between the two of them.

He lifted her against his cock and rode her hard over him. Looking down, she could see her juices covering him. She started to reach down and touch him, but he pulled her hand back quickly.

"You do that, and I'm finished. I can't wait anymore, baby. I need to be inside you. Now." Byron lifted her again and with her back against the St. Andrews, he impaled her over his shaft. She screamed.

Chapter Thirteen

Byron didn't move. Tears, fat and wet, trailed down her cheeks as she held her body rigid over him. He could feel her body adjusting to his, milking and pulling at him. He didn't want to hurt her any more. A virgin. How the hell...? She moved and he moaned before he could think. Her body was so tight and hot, he shifted slightly to relieve some of the pressure on his cock and she moaned. He moved again, this time gently rocking into her, and Taylor grabbed his shoulders and dug her nails into him.

"Please. Please, master. I need...I beg you, let me come." He looked into her eyes and he could see her pain and her need looking back at him. He rocked again and she trembled. He was so close and he knew if she came, she was going to bring him with her. He leaned forward and worried the nipple clamp with his tongue and then suckled it into his mouth. She cried out. Not from pain, but need. "Please," she sobbed.

"Come for me, Taylor. Come now." She didn't just come, she detonated.

Her body tensed for all of three seconds, then shattered around him. Her scream this time rent the air and he could hear his name as she cried it out over and over as she came. Her breasts swelled incredibly tighter and her nipples stiffened into hard peaks. When she surged against him, he realized that he hadn't moved, had forgotten to join her in her ecstasies while watching her emotions move across her face. He rocked harder into her. Over and over her body convulsed around his; her tight channel milked him and pulled him deeper into her.

He slid his hand behind her and pressed his finger into her rose bud and she came again. Every time he rocked into her, he pressed deeper into her ass. Watching her come again, he didn't feel his own climax coming up until it grabbed him by the balls and took him.

With a roar, he came hard and quick, filling her with his seed, spilling all he had within her. Then when he thought he would collapse, another powerful climax ripped over him, through him, and he surged harder into her again and again. Over and over he pumped into her; over and over he felt his cock jerk and empty inside of her.

Byron couldn't move. He knew that he should, but he was positive that he couldn't. He lifted his head, quite a feat, he thought, and looked at Taylor. Her eyes were closed and he could see her pulse pounding at her throat.

It was then that he realized that her arms were limp at her sides and that her legs no longer held him. She was unconscious. Whether from exhaustion of because she had come so hard, he didn't know, but he did smile. He could never remember rendering a woman unconscious before during sex. He gently pulled her head forward and leaned her against his shoulder. Lifting her a little higher, he moved them away from their makeshift bed and nearly staggered. Christ, he had also never felt so wobbly before either. Moving slowly, he led them to the only other door in the room and to the bed beyond. He had slept there once or twice after a good session, but never had he taken a woman there before. He laid her gently on the bed and looked down at her.

She didn't move. Moving to the other side of the bed, he pulled the blankets to the bottom and then moved the sheet wide. He went around and picked her up and then laid her on the opposite pillow and covered her up. He wanted to wake her and talk to her. He wanted to take her to the bathroom and take a long shower with her, but mostly, he wanted to crawl in beside her and pull her close. He wanted to hold her throughout the night and most of the day tomorrow if she would let him. Frowning, Byron went into the bathroom, closed the door, and looked in the mirror.

He was so fucked. He didn't know what it was about this woman, but she made him want things he didn't need. He didn't cuddle with women after sex. He sent them on their merry way, satisfied and sated. He didn't shower with them unless it was to continue what they had started, but never to soothe away their sore muscles. And he didn't take a woman's virginity. Rubbing his hand over his face, he scowled at his reflection. He was so fucked.

He went into the play room and picked up their discarded clothing. Picking up her skirt nearly made him whimper. No panties. She hadn't worn panties under this scrap of denim. He put everything, including her pack from his office, into the bath and left the bedroom, purposely not looking at the beautiful woman in his bed.

~~~

Taylor woke to a semi dark room. She didn't know where she was at first, but when she moved and pain moved through her body, she remembered. Everything. She had had sex.

Sitting up with the sheet pulled to her breasts, she looked around the room. Her eyes had adjusted now and she could make out the furniture with the light from the room right next to the bed. She assumed it was the bathroom. There wasn't a lot of furniture in the big room. There was a small desk that looked to have a new computer on it. There was a cabinet above it, closed now, and a printer on a cart. The chair was huge and looked like someone could sink into it if they wanted. There were a set of doors, sliders that she assumed was a closet, and two wingback chairs that sat to the right of the freestanding fireplace. And then the bed.

The bed was the biggest thing she had ever seen. It was a four poster that looked as if it might be old, but she knew about as much about antiques as she did anything else—very little. But it was so comfortable that she thought she might like to spend an eternity in it. That thought got her moving.

She went into the bath and was shocked at the decadence in it. The shower was huge! It looked as though several people, or two very active people, could fit inside of it. That image made her blush. There was also a garden tub with jets along most of the walls. She longed to sit in it, but remembered that this thing with Byron was for just the one night. And she had read enough romance books to know that the morning after was always uncomfortable. Instead, she reached into her pack and pulled out her baby wipes and started to clean herself up.

The blood and semen on her thighs gave her pause. She had given him her virginity. She wondered fleetingly if he noticed, and doubted it. He probably thought she was an incredibly horrible lay and wrote her off. Probably why he wasn't in bed with her. She huffed to herself. Pulling out clean panties and jeans, she started to dress. She had packed her street clothes in her bag just in case and was really glad that she had. Her breasts were sore and tender. The clamps were gone — probably thought she would steal them — and her bra hurt, but she put it on anyway thinking once she got home, she would put ice or heat on them.

The longer it took her to dress, the angrier she got. It was directed mostly at Byron, but she knew that whatever had happened between them was entirely her doing. It had been incredible and the most satisfying thing she had ever experienced, something she would think about years from now. But it was over, wham, bam, thank you ma'am; don't let the door hit you on the way out.

Moving into the play room, she felt her body respond to seeing the bench again. She would never be able to look at one again without thinking of this one night. Shaking herself mentally as well as physically, she moved to the door marked exit. It wasn't the door she had been led through last night so she assumed it was a way out.

The door spilled into a dark alley. There was one light at the end of it, just close enough to see that she wouldn't fall over anything, but too many shadows to see if there was anyone around. Pulling her coat tighter around her, she moved to the mouth of the street. It was still dark and the wind whipping around the corner nearly had her going to try and flag down a cab, but she was more determined than ever to get out of Ohio.

By the time she got to Wal-Mart at five-thirty in the morning, she wasn't only tired, but very achy as well. Her jeans rubbing against her butt reminded her with every step that he had used the flogger on her several times and very hard. Her arms hurt as well; being stretched out after so long made the muscles pull every time she reached for something. Her feet even hurt, which she couldn't imagine why. She also had the ache of having had sex for the first time. The more she walked, the more she wanted to go and soak in a big tub of hot water. Unfortunately, the Y didn't have a bathtub, only showers. By the time she had paid for her few purchases, she decided to take a cab. At this time of the morning and on a Sunday, she had no problem getting one.

On Sundays, Taylor tried to get as much done as possible. When she had lived in the apartment, she would make up her clothes, laying them out so that she need only grab a pile, shower, pull whatever was there on, and go. But she still needed to wash them. Hauling things to the Laundromat was her first order of business.

She was just putting the last load in the washer when the flipping phone rang. Looking at the caller ID, the logo for the Grant building showed up. Devin, she thought, and nearly didn't answer it. It was Sunday at seven in the morning. Did he not have better things to do than to bother her?

"You were supposed to call me last night. I waited for nearly six fucking hours and—" Taylor closed the phone. It was too early and she wasn't having the best of mornings. When it rang less than a minute later, she answered.

"Damn it, Taylor, do you—"

She hung up again. She started crying now. Never a weepy person, it made her more upset than she wanted to admit that she had had enough of the men she knew treating her like some feelingless, mindless twit. This time when the phone rang, she let him get out an entire sentence first.

"If you hang up on me again, so help me Christ, I will find you and beat your ass."

The phone closed again. She was nearly sobbing now and turned her back to the woman in the Laundromat with her. She didn't think he would call her again, but send out the police or the National Guard, so when the phone rang again; she seriously debated on chucking the thing in the washing machine.

"Hello, sweetheart. It's Ronnie. Devin has given up. Well, for now anyway. He so hates when someone hangs up on him, but I told him he was being very rude to you."

Taylor couldn't help it. She burst into sobbing tears. She didn't know how long her crying jag went on, but when she blew her nose again and put the phone back to her ear, she wondered if Ronnie had hung up.

"Hello?"

"Oh, Taylor, honey, are you all right? Why don't you let Devin come and get you and bring you here? I promise he'll not say a single word to you; I'll gag him if you want me to. I know you've been very stressed and all. Come over and visit me, please? Devin is making me insane since I got home from the hospital and if I can't get up then someone needs to help me plot to have him murdered. I'm betting that you have lots of ideas on how to do that too."

"No, but thanks. I have stuff to do today. It's just been a...I've been feeling sorry for myself and...well, it's not entirely his fault that I'm crying." Taylor wasn't sure which him she was thinking about, but let it go for now.

"All the more reason for you to come here. I'm a great listener. I know that this thing with the Feds has you upset and I'm sure whatever happened between you and Jamie can't be helping. Come here, please? Oh damn! The family dinner...that's okay, you can go too. You know most of us now..."

"No offense, Ronnie, but no, and hell no. I have laundry do to and I have to get some emails answered. Tell your husband that I'll be at this office tomorrow after work. I really don't think I can handle one more shitty thing happening to me today. I will even be civil to the Feds too. Please?"

"Yes. All right. I'll make him understand. You have my cell phone number in your phone. If you just want to talk or bitch about the Grant men, then call. I'm sure any one of us Grant women would be more than glad to listen." Taylor could hear someone talking in the background and wondered what Devin was thinking about Ronnie's statement.

After hanging up, Taylor sat and watched her clothes swirl around the dryer. It wasn't just the Feds or Jamie that had her weepy. Byron did as well. He had done just what he said he would, fuck her. She told him that it was just for one night and never again. What had she expected, roses, words of undying love, him to beg her to never leave him? No, she didn't expect it, but something would have been nice.

Chapter Fourteen

Byron hung up the phone. Again. Where the hell was she? He had called the number Taylor had given on her application twelve times since nine o'clock. It was just after one now.

When he had gone back to the bedroom at ten to wake her and get her on her way, he discovered that she was gone—all her clothes and her bag as well. When he went out the exit at the back of the playroom, he could see her tiny feet prints in the snow moving out to the street and that, for some reason, made him madder.

He had wanted her to leave, so why the hell was he so pissed off that she had? And why was he trying to call her? Did he want to fight with her over the phone? Because he knew without a doubt that was exactly what they would do if he were to find her. He hadn't had to listen to her reasons for him to let her stay with him—he had every scenario worked out. What her pleas would be and his answers for her. He had hardened his heart against her tears and what he would say about those as well. Damn it, she was supposed to beg him to stay!

And what the hell was she thinking leaving in the middle of the night anyway? Did she want to get mugged? Or raped for that matter? Was she so stupid that she...no, not stupid, so stubborn that she would risk her life rather than let him take her home? Damned woman, he was going to beat her ass when he found her. He was reaching out to pick up the phone on his desk again when it rang.

"You had better have a good fucking reason for leaving my bed." When silence answered him, he leaned forward and closed his eyes when he saw who was on his caller ID.

"But you were so kind to me last night. Whatever reason would I have to leave a big, powerful, manly man like you? I was just so overwhelmed by all your masculinity," the syrupy sweet voice answered.

"Fuck off, Spencer. I thought you were someone else. What do you want anyway?" Byron barked back.

"I should hope so! I was wondering if Meggie could ride with you today. She said she wants to spend some time with you. She misses you for some stupid reason."

"Yeah, that'll be fine. I have that car seat from before. Is it still the right size for her now that she's six?"

"Should be, but I'll bring the one from my car with me and you can keep it if it's not. Hum, O'Malley wants to know if you're bringing anyone with you. She said to tell you if you have a date, then Meggie would understand."

"I do have a date, with Meggie. Tell your wife to stay out of it. Taylor and I are not a couple. When will you be here?"

"Around two-thirty. And I am not saying that to my wife. She'll hurt me." Laughing, Spencer hung up.

Did he want to be a couple with Taylor? Did he want to spend time with her, even outside the playroom back at the club? Yeah, he realized he did. She was a handful and she was an aggravation, but damn, she was fun.

He picked up the phone in his home office again and dialed the number. He couldn't even leave a voice message for her. It just continued to ring and ring. He was going to have a talk with her about having a cell phone for emergencies.

Byron sat there and thought about having her last night. Christ, she was delicious. Her body had responded to his in ways he had never connected with anyone before. And her taste—sweet honey and cream had filled his mouth when he had tasted her. Even her nipples responded in ways no other woman's had. He wanted her again, not just for the playroom. He wanted to take her to his bed here in his home and make love to her, slow and easy.

Her virginity had been a surprise. Hell, if he was honest with himself, it had been a major turn on for him knowing that no other man had been where he had been, never been deep inside of her. He couldn't believe that someone as beautiful and responsive as she was hadn't had another man sample what he had — paradise on long silky legs. He glanced at the clock.

Great, he had just over an hour to try and get his hormones back under control. He snorted when he thought of what Spencer or even Cait would say if Byron came downstairs with a hard-on. He knew that he would never hear the end of it.

~~~

Taylor went back to her room and put her things away. She got her stuff ready for work then sat down and finished her letter of resignation to the Freedoms. She was going to e-mail it to them first thing Monday morning. She was so exhausted. She had had enough and closed down her document program and crawled into the bed. Taylor barely got the covers up over her before she was sound asleep. It was just after seven o'clock in the evening.

It had turned bitterly cold overnight. Her coat, at best a jacket, kept very little of the wind from touching her skin beneath it while she walked to the office early the next morning. By the time she was stamping the snow off her feet, she was frozen. She went to the break area and microwaved a cup of water so that she could have a nice cup of hot tea before she got things started. The power flickered twice but then it was fine.

Taylor was sitting at her desk, having just got her computer out and sent her email to her bosses when the power danced again. She held her breath, hoping that it would go off for good and hoping that it wouldn't. Before she could try to figure out why she was so conflicted, the power went off again. Damn and goody raced through her head. Damn — another day short of pay, and goody — now I can go home and go back to bed.

She waited for an hour and decided she wasn't turning herself into a popsicle for anyone and was going home. She just remembered that she had promised Devin she would be there after work. Damn, damn, and double damn. She pulled out the dreaded cell and called the office.

"Hello, this is Taylor Bennett. May I speak to Mr. Grant please?" She had hoped they would be closed down due to the power thing too, but the secretary answered on the third ring.

113

"Oh, lord, you'll have to do better than that. There's the doctor one here that's a real doctor, the one that makes all sorts of money, and the one that's the lawyer. You know a first name?"

"Devin. And I'm pretty sure they're all doctors—real ones. Is he in by any chance?"

"Oh, that one. No, he's off with the wife to a doctor's appointment. Nothing serious, just a checkup after she had her baby. That other one, the money maker, I'd like to have me some of that—the man, not the money. He's out with his wife too. I guess I'd like to have the money too. Girl can't have too much of that, can she? Anyway, did you know she was an ex-con? And her being pretty and all."

Taylor couldn't believe the indiscretion of this woman. She wanted to tell her so, but decided that it really wasn't any of Taylor's business. She did make a mental note to herself to tell the Grants—Devin and Ronnie—that she would appreciate it if Donna didn't have access to her files, thank you very much.

"Yeah, okay. I have an appointment with them when I get off work and there is no power here, so do you think it would be all right if I came in now?"

"Oh sure, honey. You come on in. If they aren't here, you and I can visit. I get really bored listening to these people whine about their crap all day long."

Taylor hung up and gathered up her stuff. Sheesh, she wondered, where did they find that one? That woman wouldn't know how to keep a secret if her life depended on it, Taylor was sure.

"I have to run down to the corner deli for my lunch. Do you think you could maybe watch things for a minute or two? I'll pick you up something if you want."

Taylor had been at the Grant office for just over two hours waiting for someone to call back, Donna said. And the woman hadn't shut up once. Taylor's head was swimming with pain and she was sure she was going to have permanent damage done to her eyes they had bugged so much. She now knew more about each Grant in the building, including spouses, than she bet any of them knew about each other.

"Yeah, go ahead. I'm not sure what they have, but if you could pick me up a veggie tray thing, that'll be great, and a water." Taylor wasn't hungry; it was only a little after eleven, but the quicker Donna left, the quicker there would be peace and quiet in the room.

As soon as the elevator closed, the phone started ringing. Taylor wasn't sure if she should answer it, but what if it was Devin? She would simply answer it and then tell whoever called that the Grants would be back if it wasn't him.

At two, Taylor realized that the stupid woman had been gone for three hours. Taylor didn't even notice the time fly by; the phone hadn't stopped ringing and people had been in and out the whole time. It had taken her three phone calls to realize that Donna was supposed to be answering the phone for both the law firm and the financial firm. Taylor wasn't sure how the woman thought it was boring working here. Taylor was actually having a good time. Most of the time at the Freedom Fighters, she would answer three, maybe five calls a day. Here, she had taken around twenty messages and the phone hadn't stopped.

"Grant Corporation, how my I help you?" Taylor was trying to hook the printer up to her laptop. She had a really nice program on it that she typed messages on and was going to transcribe the messages she took to that then print them.

"Donna, are my sons about? I don't care at the moment which one, I just need to speak to one of them, please."

"No, ma'am, no one is here but me. And it's Taylor Bennett, not Donna. Is there anything I can help you with?" Taylor was suddenly sorry she had started answering the phone.

"Well, hello, my dear. It's Margaret Parker, the boys' mother. You should have come to dinner yesterday. We missed you. I know that Byron did. Are you working there now? I hadn't heard that."

"No, that stup...Donna went to lunch and hasn't returned yet. I'm expecting her any moment." Closing her eyes, Taylor hoped that Mrs. Parker didn't notice her flub. Of course that would be too easy.

"No, dear, you had it right, stupid about describes her. How long has the idiot been gone today? The other week she went to the bank and didn't return for four hours. The bank is across the street.

I don't know what her excuse was, but Nicky said he needs someone to work the desk and she is a warm body until he finds someone."

"She left here around eleven. I don't know where the deli is, but that is where she was headed. She sure can empty her head faster than anyone I've ever met. Christ, the things she says to strangers! Anyway, can I do anything for you?"

"Yes, I was wondering if you could get into that filing cabinet across from you. I'll give you the combination. I need to find out who that woman was at table four at the banquet. She had that horrible head dress on that looked like an ostrich crapped on her head."

"Mrs. Durk. She has a specialty shop on Hudson. I think her first name is Carol, but I'm sure that's who you mean." Taylor stood as she told the older woman ready for her to give Taylor the combo.

"Yes! That's it. Oh my, this is wonderful. How did you know that? I've been racking my head for two days. Morgan brought her up the other day and I've been trying to think of it since."

"I have a knack for names. I don't know why. I have a hard time...hum, the phone is ringing. Do you think I should keep answering? I don't want to seem forward about doing it, but it just seemed silly to let it keep ringing."

"Oh no, dear, you go ahead. I'm sure that my sons will be very happy. I'll talk to you later. Have a good day, and thanks."

At four-thirty, Taylor was exhausted. But it was a good kind of exhaustion. She had been busy nonstop all day and she never once felt too much out of her depth. She was on the speaker phone with the tech support guy she had found the number for in the desk. She was currently under the desk trying to do what he told her about hooking up the printer.

"So I have the white wire and the blue one. Where did you say to put them? And be nice." His name was Derek and he had made her laugh several times with his flamboyant ways.

"Honey, that's so not white. It's euchre, or maybe a soft shell white at best. It goes into the box you hooked up to your computer. It's the outlet marked blush-rose. Insert it in there."

Blush- rose? There was pink or blue; she put it in the pink one. She heard the elevator open and shouted that she would be right with them; she was a little tied up.

"Okay. Now what? Oh, wait, this blue one will go in the blue one, right?" She smiled, knowing he would have another name for the blue.

"Well if you want to be passé about it, it's blue. But I think it's more of a cerulean or maybe an aquamarine. Yes, go ahead and put the blue in the blue outlet." She laughed out loud at his pouty tone and she came out from under the desk. She fell into the chair when she saw who as standing just on the other side.

"Hello, Taylor. What the hell do you think you're doing?" Byron asked her.

Chapter Fifteen

Byron couldn't believe it when they stepped off the elevator and Taylor shouted for them to hang on. They didn't see her, but Devin pointed to the phone and that's when Derek started talking.

Devin had told him yesterday at his mom's that Taylor was going to be at his office this evening and that he should come in town and have lunch with them all. He could then come by the office and speak to her afterwards. Christmas was just a few days away and Byron could stay with him for a few days rather than drive all the way back to his house then back again a few days later to be at Mom's for Christmas. Lunch had turned into shopping and then shopping had turned into drinks afterwards.

"What, pray tell, are you doing under the desk? And where the hell is that stupid secretary of mine? She was supposed to be here answering phones," Nickolas said. He winked at Taylor and then opened the door to his office.

"Donna? Oh, she...she went to get lunch. She said she'd be right back. I have messages for you both as soon as they're done printing." The printer spit out the last sheet as soon as she finished talking.

She separated them out and handed each man, Devin and Nicky, their stack. She had color coded them, Byron saw, according to department. There were four messages on each sheet and each man had at least ten sheets each it looked like. Taylor wasn't anything if not organized. Devin looked over his notes and then handed them to his wife. Nickolas stared at his sheets as if she had just handed him something precious.

"Are you all right? Anyway, I wasn't sure if I should answer the phone, but I was afraid if you called back, then I wouldn't be able to tell you I was here. Then when you kept not calling, I thought I should keep answering. You're mother said it was all right. I'm really sorry if I—" The phone rang again. She looked at each man and Devin nodded as if to say, "are you going to answer that?"

"Grant Corporation. How may I...it's Donna. She said she forgot to come back to work. How the heck did... How the heck do you forget to come back to work, you twit? I've been here all...I don't really give a rat's turd what you bought me. You left me here all day...oh yeah, that's really what I meant, for you to go all over the city to get me carrot sticks... No, I don't care to pay you back. I didn't eat them and I...hum, she hung up."

Nickolas threw back his head and laughed. Devin was hanging onto the desk and laughing as well. Morgan and Ronnie were sitting in the lounge chairs snickering and holding their sides. Byron wasn't amused.

"So, instead of being at your work like you were supposed to, you've been here answering the phone and taking messages. I've been trying to call you since you left my bed on Sunday morning. Do you have any idea how worried I've been? Anything could have happened to you when you left like a thief in the night, slipping out the back door and running the streets at God knows what hour of the morning. I should—"

"Now you listen here, you unmitigated jackass. What I do, where I do it, and fucking who I do it with is not any of your business. I have never met a more nosey bunch of...I told you when I had sex with you that it was a onetime deal. You agreed. Besides, I didn't see your naked ass lying there all concerned about me. So fuck the hell off."

His temper snapped. "Well, maybe I want to make it my business. Have you ever thought of that? Huh? And that's another thing! How the hell did you make it this long in your life and still be a virgin? You should have told me! Christ, I could have hurt you and what the hell would have happened then, huh? Did you ever thing that—"

"Are you even listening to yourself? Are you insane? I thought hurting me was the fucking point. And when was I supposed to tell you? When you had me strapped to your bench flogging me or when you had your dick in my mouth. You didn't seem to have any problems with my virginity then. Why the hell should it be one now?" She was gathering up her things.

"Where the hell do you think you're going? Is that what I can expect from you, running off every time you get your panties in a twist? We aren't even close to being finished here yet. I have more to say to you and I'm going to say it."

He knew the moment he grabbed her arm that he had made a mistake. Her fist connected with his nose so fast he didn't have time to even brace for it. And if that didn't hurt enough, she brought her knee up and kicked him square in the family jewels. The few seconds it took to register pain, he used that time to realize that she was as beautiful in her anger as she was when she came. But it was the voice behind him that had him curl into a tight ball on the floor, the one that could make him feel five years old faster than anyone in the world could. She also apparently had the added power to keep Taylor from blasting him more. Thankfully. But not keep her from leaving.

"So, Byron Kelly Grant, you took a woman's virginity. Are you planning to do anything about this, or are you going to argue with her like a fish monger in your brother's office?"

He looked over at her as he cupped his groin. Pain raced all over his body in ten seconds flat. "Hello, Mom."

Margaret went to the phone and dialed. Byron could only hope she was hiring a hit man to end his misery. But he was reasonably sure she would let him suffer first.

"Hello, David, It's Margaret Parker. There is a nice young lady coming down...Yes, that would be her. Could you please have Miss Bennett wait for me? Tell her that the...hold on for a second, David. Devin, what did Taylor call Byron?"

"I believe she called him an 'unmitigated jackass,' Mom."

Byron decided if he didn't die, Devin was going to.

"Yes, that's it. Tell her that the unmitigated jackass and his brothers are not coming with us...Yes, tell her I see it, and that it will be my pleasure to bring it to her." She hung up the phone and huffed at him. Byron was sure that he was going to pay for this for the rest of his life.

"We are going to take that poor girl to dinner. I would imagine that since she had been stuck here in this office all day, she didn't get food. Devin, you'll pack up the computer and she said to tell you she might be back. Is it important that she come back tonight?"

"Yes, it is. I can't go into the case, but she has a meeting tonight at seven. She's blown this off several times, so I really need her here."

"She strikes me as a very responsible young woman, regardless of the company she keeps." Her pointed look at Byron didn't go unnoticed. "Don't think, young man, that I'm finished with you either. You'll be here when we return."

As soon as all the women left, Spencer whooped with laughter, Nickolas called Damon and told him that he needed to come up quick, that Byron had his nose broken by a woman and his nuts needed to be lowered back down to his groin. Devin was laughing so hard that Byron hoped he keeled over and hit his own nose.

~~~

Taylor was pacing when the elevator opened finally. She nearly turned and left the very nice lobby when she saw them get off. Sheesh, did these people do everything in packs? Mrs. Parker was leading the way and the other women were right behind her. They all looked as if they had been laughing.

She flushed when she remembered what she had said to Byron. It wasn't like her to lose her temper, but he made her so angry. Taylor wondered how long Margaret had been standing there and how much she had heard. Not that it mattered. In a few days, she would be gone anyway.

"Hello, dear. You must be starved. I know I am. Do you like Chinese? I just love it. That's where we're taking you, and don't bother trying to get out of it. Caitlynne is going to join us and we're all going to talk about how horrible of a mother I am and how much it would cost to have my sons murdered in their sleep."

Taylor burst out laughing. She really liked this woman. She rarely had friends in her life and never one that made her feel worthy like Margaret did. Even with Taylor cussing like a sailor on a three day pass, she still treated her nicely. They were just being seated when Cait showed up.

"I just spoke to Grant. He said that you broke Byron's nose and probably his privates as well. Not that I don't think he probably deserved it, but he really is a nice guy. Not a nice as Spencer, but nice."

"No, he's not, but it's nice of you to say. He thinks he owns me because we had sex. Stupid man. I told him that it was just a one nighter, but now he's become all possessive. I don't need a keeper, thanks. Besides, I'll be leaving soon anyway."

"Leaving? You can't leave! Good heavens, Taylor, you are involved in a major case. You can't possibly think the Feds are going to...shit!" Ronnie turned a bright red and suddenly started fussing with her daughter.

"There are Feds investigating your case? Why? I mean, really, once we shut the place down there won't be any more problems from them. That guy has apparently done this kind of thing before and it was easy enough to get others, men and women, to come forward once the article ran in the Dispatch," Cait said as she broke open her spring roll. It wasn't until no one made a comment that she looked up. "What?"

"Hum, two different cases. The one you're referring to is the...the bite marks. Ronnie is talking about something else I got myself mixed up in. Something that I seriously wish I would have ignored. I'm not staying and there is no way in hell they can make me."

"Actually, they can. And probably will. You are the prime witness and they need you to bring these guys down. Don't be surprised if they tell you the same thing tonight. I wouldn't mess with them, Taylor. Maybe you can work for the Freedoms just until this is over."

"The Freedoms? You mean those guys that advertise on the local station 'no case is too big, we'll fight for your freedom because we are the Freedom Fighters?' Sheesh, they're corny. What on earth could you be mixed up with...good heavens; you're not dating them, are you? No wonder Byron was pissed." Morgan had done a perfect imitation of their commercial and made the people at the next table laugh. Taylor didn't watch too much television, and was now thankful that she had missed that one.

"Byron is pissed for other reasons. And he'll soon figure out that I may be a su...I may be different outside the bedroom than when I am in it. I don't care what he says." Taylor looked at the other women at the table when it got eerily quiet. None of them would look at her.

"Honey, you can say it. Submissive. And I'm guessing that you are only a sexual one, not a lifestyle sub. Hum, I would imagine that Byron, as a dominant, would want to think he can order you around. Don't let him. He needs to be shook up now and again. Oh don't look at me like that, Morgan Grant. Did you think I didn't know he owns that lovely club on High Street? I'm his mother, aren't I?"

"I don't think...I was under the impression...does Byr know you know about...his, how shall I say, sexual preferences? Because I'm pretty sure he thinks you don't." Morgan grinned as she asked her mother-in-law.

"I have no idea. Nor do I care. Now, Taylor, I do have a question I'd like to ask you, if you don't mind. Tell me what a ball gag is and what it's used for." The table erupted in laughter.

Taylor didn't understand, but didn't see any problem telling the elderly woman everything she asked. Taylor did wonder, however, if she had been storing up the questions for some time, because she seemed to have a lot of them. By the time they were finished eating, it was past time to get back to the office.

Morgan sat in the back seat with her on the way back. "I'm not sure what you are planning, but Nickolas told me to offer you whatever you want to come and work for him. He said whatever. If you knew my husband, you'd be surprised. He's the tightest man I've ever met when it comes to money. Well, except for the boys and me. I once saw him berate Byron for three days because there was a twenty-eight cent mistake on his checking account and he wouldn't call the bank and demand an audit."

"I'm moving back to my home state. I'm not cut out for here. But I thank you. I've been...I don't belong here. I need to try and start again, sort of become someone no one knows about. Understand?"

"Yes, I can understand, but it doesn't work. Trust me, Taylor, I know. And if Byron has anything to say about—"

"He doesn't. I was a quick lay, nothing more. And I would appreciate it if you would just let it go. There is nothing between the two of us, only mutual sexual gratification." Taylor looked up in the rearview mirror in time to catch Margaret looking at her strangely.

Taylor wasn't staying. They couldn't make her; at least, she didn't think they could. If they wanted her help, then they would have to play by her rules. They pulled up in front of the building and talk about what may or may not happen in the Grant offices came to an end, at least for the moment.

There were three Federal Agents there when Taylor stepped off the elevator. Also, there was Devin and another woman Taylor didn't know, Nickolas, and Byron. The only person she saw was the latter man.

"Before you begin, I'd like a word with Taylor please. I promise this won't take long." He walked slowly to her.

Taylor could see that his nose was swollen and his eyes had the beginnings of bruises under them. She really had broken his nose. She felt bad, but would do it all over again if he thought she was a push over. When he was within several inches of her, she looked up at him. Christ, the man was an Adonis. She didn't know whether to touch him or run from him.

"Byron, these men really need to talk to—"

"Give him a few minutes, Devin. I believe he does have a few things to say to her before I have my own little talk with him." Taylor glanced over at Margaret and glared. Damn it to hell, did everyone have it out for her?

She led him to Nickolas' office and waited while he shut the door. She was suddenly nervous and she wanted to pace. She noticed that she did that a lot lately and wondered why. Then he moved closer and she took a step back. He kept advancing; she kept retreating until she hit the desk behind her.

"How does your ass feel? Is it tender still?" His whispered question made her moan. It was out before she could stop it. "I'll take that as a yes. I'm sorry I grabbed you. I'm sorry that I yelled at you. I had all these things I wanted to say to you. I was going to wow you with my apologies. But now that you're here, all I can think about was having you the other night. The way your body fit under mine and the way you tasted on my tongue. My cock sliding down the back of your throat when you sucked me... Christ, I've had to jerk off four times in the last twenty-four hours just to be able to remember to breathe right. Will you, Taylor, will you let me kiss you?"

Her own breathing was difficult and her pulse was pounding. She didn't want him; she didn't need him either. But her body had other ideas. Her hand, the treacherous thing, reached up and curled itself around his neck and pulled him toward her mouth.

Chapter Sixteen

Byron moved slowly, wanting to savor her. His heart had nearly leapt out of his chest when she touched him. But he still moved slowly. He wasn't blowing his chance to be close to her again. She moved a step forward and he wrapped his arms around her and gathered her to him. Taylor felt wonderful in his arms, warm and soft. When he felt himself wanting to press her down on the desk and take her, he pulled back. He smiled when she whimpered.

"Taylor, come home with me tonight. I want to make love to you in a bed. I want to feel you wrapped around me again. Maybe if we get this out of our systems, we can move on with our lives, don't you think?" She stiffened and pulled away.

He let her go. It was hard, but he also took a step back from her. His cock ached and when she glanced down at it, he nearly groaned. He was too busy trying to not pounce on her to notice that she was pissed.

"Tell me, Byron, is that the only thing you think with? I told you, no more. I want you to stay away from me. I'm sure that once I'm gone, you'll be able to work me out of your system, as you put it, without any problems. The notches on your bed will grow exponentially then. If you'll excuse me, I have things to do."

He didn't grab her this time—he wasn't completely stupid—but he did step in front of her—from a distance. "Damn it, I'm trying to say I want you. What the hell is wrong with being honest about it?"

"Oh, I have no problems with you being honest, but don't begrudge me for being so as well. I don't want you. I don't want you near me, touching me or inside me. Leave. Me. Alone. Clear enough for you?"

She stormed past him and out the door. He rubbed his chest. He felt like something important had just happened and he wasn't so sure it was a good thing. Frowning, he sat in the chair and looked after where she had gone. He didn't even see his mother walk in several minutes later. Nor did he realize she was there. It wasn't until he looked at her that he realized she was smiling.

"Well, what have you figured out? You know, of all my sons, I knew that it would be the hardest for you. You never needed anyone, not even me most of the time. And before you deny it, let me finish. You were seven when I realized it for myself. Your father knew right from the start. I'm a little slower I guess. It was when you fell from the tree in the front yard, do you remember it?"

"Yes. I was trying to get the paper airplane that Dad had given me. We had made it together and he let me draw the design on it. And I do need you. Every day of my life."

"You're a sweet boy. But what happened that day, Byron? Do you remember? What did you do when you fell?"

"Mom, I've gone over this with you before. It was just silly for me to walk all the way home in order for you to take me all the way back to the hospital when I was less than a mile from there. I got there just fine and they set my arm. What does that have to do with this?" He wasn't sure what any of this meant, and was glad she didn't ask him.

"You wouldn't let them call me until they had made sure it was broken. You told them if it was just a bruise that I'd tan your hide for making a big deal out of nothing. As it was, I didn't get there until you were nearly plastered up."

"Yes, and if I remember correctly, you still tanned my hide. Mom, why are you bringing up a broken arm that happened over twenty years ago?"

She smiled at him. It wasn't a smile that he liked seeing on her. It was sad and seemed bittersweet to him. And he could see the tears starting to gather in her eyes. Before he could move forward in his chair to take her into his arms, she stood. So did he.

"Taylor can make you the happiest man on earth if you'd let her. She isn't stupid, nor is she a freak like she seems to think she is. And as a partner, I see great things for the two of you if you set your minds to it. If you love this girl, then you'd be a fool to let her go. When you figure it out, let me know."

Byron dropped back into the chair. Love her? Hardly. She made his life a living hell most of the time. He had never met a more contrary, stubborn woman in his life. Love her? He would just as soon never love if loving Taylor Bennett felt like this. She was opinioned and sexy and had a body...no, he meant that she had a mean streak down her back...he had hurt her. He couldn't really blame her for defending herself when he had started it. He rubbed his chest again. He didn't love her. He simply wanted her. That was all. His mother had it wrong, just like him not needing her. That was just silly; he loved his mother and needed her.

He stood again and walked out of Nicky's office. Love her indeed. He was nearly home when he realized that all he had been thinking about was Taylor. He decided that he had had enough, wasting time on a woman that wanted nothing to do with him. When he got home, he turned on the television—really loud. Of course he couldn't love Taylor. They would probably kill each other within a week if they were together.

He found himself not knowing what was going on with the program that was on and turned the TV off. He looked around his house. He had bought it several years ago because he needed the extra space to work.

The house was beautifully decorated. He had paid a fortune for someone to come in and make it look "homey." She had done a good job, but he knew that it didn't have the same feelings he got at his mom's house or at either of his married brothers. There was the usual furniture—couch, love seat, coffee table, and lamps. But the room lacked sticky finger marks on the end tables and toys on the floor. The kitchen was state of the art with every new appliance known to man, but he couldn't remember the last thing he had cooked in it. He had used the microwave to heat stuff up, but hadn't cooked anything since right after he bought it. The bedrooms were the same way. Well, except for his bedroom. There, he was at home in his house. The bed was made for his tall frame and the mattress was thick and firm. His furniture had been a gift from his mother now that he remembered and it was perfect for him—large and heavy, clean lines and straight angles. He realized it wasn't a home, but a house.

The building out back was nearly seventeen thousand square feet of work area and a shipping dock as well. He spent more of his time there than in the house. He had even had a cot put in there and a small kitchen. That place reflected more of him than this house. He wondered what Taylor would think of his house. He wondered if she would make it a home.

~~~

"Miss Bennett, you are simply not listening. You cannot leave that job. We are launching a major investigation on information that you've provided us. You leaving would be dangerous to both you and the mission. At this point, I will take measures to make sure you cooperate."

Agent Felix Fenton had been talking at her for the past three hours. No matter what she said, he wouldn't listen. Devin had long since given up on trying to plead with her, and Nickolas had gone home frustrated and a little pissed off. She still wasn't sure what he had to do with any of this, but right now she didn't care.

"What are you going to do, put me in jail, prison? Gee, won't that get me fired? I have given you everything I have on this stupid thing. I've been cooperative—okay, I've been semi-cooperative. I'm leaving here on Christmas Eve and by Christmas morning, I plan to be on the beach walking along the shore. I'm going home. I have to work out my two weeks' notice and I need the money."

"Two weeks' notice? What...are you saying you've already given your notice? When? For Christ's sake, woman, are you out of your mind? They'll kill you."

"For quitting? I hardly think so. Good night, gentlemen." She started to put on her coat when the agent stood. He looked determined. Taylor took a step back and then suddenly Cait was between them.

"I'll see her home. She'll be staying tonight with us. Come along, Taylor. And if you don't, I will arrest you." Taylor started to argue, but then just shook her head. She was tired and she wanted to go to bed. Kill her indeed. She went into the outer office and noticed that all the lights were off. He had gone home.

"Taylor, I'm afraid I have to agree with the agent. The amount of money they're talking? It could be very hazardous to your wellbeing. I think you should go in tomorrow and tell them that you've changed your mind about quitting."

She didn't answer. She wasn't really listening anyway. Byron had left. But then she didn't know why that should surprise her. She wasn't going to have sex with him anymore so he had done what she had asked him to.

"The Freedoms could care less about me. They barely come into the office anymore anyway. He said that he wanted to get me out of his system. Why would a man say that to a woman?"

"I'm not sure. How often do they come in together, you think? Once or twice a week, or more, do you think?"

"Less, maybe twice a month. I see them singly at least three times a week, but seldom together. I told him when we had sex the first time that it would be the only time. I thought he'd be happy to have me not clinging to him. I don't understand men, do you?"

"I'm not an expert on them, no. But Byron is a nice guy. He works hard and he's a fantastic artist." Taylor looked out the window.

She wasn't an expert either. But she did know that she wanted to get away from him. She didn't think she could take any more heartache from the Grant men. But the thought of spending another night with Byron made her heart race and her body weep for him. She wanted him, but more, she needed him. He made her feel things that she had never felt for anyone before.

"He asked me to go home with him tonight. He said that he wanted to make love to me so that he could get me out of his system, so that he could get on with his life...so that we could get on with our lives. Maybe he's right. He...Cait, could you take me to his house? Now, I mean?"

Maybe she was making the biggest mistake of her life. Maybe. But she also knew that in a few days, she would be gone and then he truly would be out of her life as well. Cait turned off the highway and handed Taylor her cell. She waited for him to answer.

"It's Taylor Bennett. Can I still come over?" Taylor said in way of greeting. He didn't answer for several seconds and she was sure he was going to say no.

131

"Yes. I'd like that very much. Do you need me to come and get you? Are you still at the office?"

"No. Cait said she'd bring me there. I have to be at work at eight-thirty in the morning. Will you be all right to take me?"

"Yes. I'll make sure you get to work on time. Tell Cait I'm at my house in town. She'll know where it is."

"All right. I'll...I guess I'll see you in a little while." She hung up without waiting for his reply.

In ten minutes, she was standing in front of his house. Byron was standing there waiting for her. He was dressed in a pair of jeans and some boots and nothing else. It was a wonder he wasn't freezing. As soon as Cait's car door closed behind her, he was pulling her into his arms and his mouth was crushed over hers.

His chilled body warmed then heated more under her fingers as she touched him. Her body seemed to come alive under his touch. His mouth moved along her jaw to her neck and he nipped her gently at first, then more firmly. She moaned and returned his nips with more of her own. He had her coat unbuttoned and he was hard as stone when he pressed against her.

"Come inside before Cait has us arrested for public nudity. Besides, the neighborhood doesn't need to see me make love to you on my front lawn." He took her hand and led her to the open door.

The door shut behind her and he pulled her close again. His kisses were hotter and more demanding. When his cold hands reached under her shirt to cup her breasts, she startled back.

"Sorry. Maybe we should slow down a bit. At least until I have a chance to warm my fingers up. The rest of me is already on fire. Go into the living room. There's a fire going in the grate. I'll just be a minute; I want to turn off the oven." She took off her coat and he hung it in the hall closet.

"You know how to cook? I can barely boil water. There isn't anything to cook with where I live, so I mostly eat out." She started to follow him to the kitchen and stopped.

She was here for sex, not a cooking lesson. She started to back away and go where he had told her, but he took her hand and led her to the kitchen. The place was magnificent.

All the appliances were stainless steel and sparkled under the bright lights. The counters and the island were tile, bright whites and deep blues. The glass fronted cabinets were lit from the inside with wood that was painted a glossy white. The floor, also tiled, picked up the same pattern on the back splash of the counters and the curtains and placemats on the bar. She marveled at the smaller appliances; a large, odd-looking coffee maker and mixer were in use. There was also a huge crock on the island filled with wooden spoons and wire whisks and anything else he might need.

"I was making myself some pancakes and bacon. Would you like to join me? I have plenty. I also have links and coffee if you want," he said as he measured out the flour into the mixing bowl.

"I don't think I could eat anything, thanks. This is beautiful. I've never been in a better equipped kitchen. My aunt Isadora had a smallish kitchen and she wasn't much of a cook. I never learned how." She sat on one of the bar stools and watched him. He poured her a glass of iced tea and set it in front of her.

"That's unsweetened. I don't drink tea myself, but Cait and Spencer were here a few days ago, and that's all she drinks. If you need sugar, I've only the real stuff, not artificial." She declined both. Her first sip told her that it was brewed and not the instant kind.

While he finished cooking his dinner, they talked. If she had to tell anyone what they talked about, she would say nothing. He told her about his experiences in the kitchen and she told him about her life living with a maiden aunt on a farm in the middle of nowhere.

"She had these geese that hated me. Every time I went out into the yard, one of them would herd me toward the others until they had me trapped. Then they would beat me with their wings until I fell to the ground. I swear to this day that goose is still waiting for me to come back so it can have another go at me."

"How old were you? I can almost see you running across the yard, dark pigtails bouncing behind you with these demented geese nipping at your heels."

"I was eight. And I did have pigtails. My aunt was very strict and she wouldn't let me cut my hair. I think by the time I was nineteen, my hair reached down to my knees. The day after she died, I went to the barber in town and had him whack it all off. He was grinning the whole time he did it. No one cared for the way

Isadora was raising me, but then, when she's all you have..." She shrugged.

"My brother Damon had this stupid cat. I mean, it really was stupid. It would actually fall in its milk while eating. I swear there were times it didn't know where its dish was unless Damon picked him up and sat him in front of it. Anyway, this cat, his name was Pock. I'm not sure now why, but I'm sure Damon does. Pock would follow us out to the garage every morning when Mom took us to school and it would still be there when we came home. One morning, Mom put the door down as she always did and left. She was gone for probably six hours that day. When she returned, the stupid cat was under the garage door, his head and paws hanging out from under the door."

"Oh, no! That poor thing; she killed it. Damon must have been devastated."

Byron came around to her side of the bar and hugged her from behind. "No, the cat was fine. When she lifted the door back up, he laid there for a few seconds and she thought for sure he was a goner. Then he just stretched out and stood up. She said he looked up at her as if to say, 'where the hell have you been all day?' and then proceeded to lick himself clean. Every once in a while, he would look at her, but he continued to clean himself up. He wouldn't go in the garage anymore and when my mom started a car, he would run like hell to hide under the house."

He leaned in and kissed her as he finished the story. His voice had been getting lower the closer he got to her and when he turned her around, he was nearly whispering. His hands were gentle along her jaw and his mouth was hot against hers.

"Taylor, I want you. I want to take you upstairs to my bed and ravage you. But I don't know if I can wait that long. I want to be inside of you in the worst way, love."

"Yes. I want you too. Please, Byron." He lifted her and sat her on the counter in front of them and she wrapped her legs around him as he kissed her again.

Chapter Seventeen

Taylor tasted of the sweet syrup she had taken off his plate. Her skin smelled of warm kitchen and the scent that was unique to her, fresh and herbal. Byron was sure all he could smell was her soap and none of the heavy perfumes that most women of his acquaintances wore. She wore no makeup and he realized that he liked not having to worry about smearing or mussing her. Her clothes were not designer, but sturdy and warm, comfortable and soft. Like her.

Kissing her was a wonder as well. Her mouth was firm and soft, her lips wet from the moisture of her tongue, not some gloss that hid her taste. Her tongue slid along his as if it belonged and knew him. When she moaned, it was because of her enjoyment and not because she thought it was what he wanted to hear. She was purely without an ulterior motive; she wanted him and nothing more. Her hands felt good on his body, his skin. She moved along him, touching him gently here and tighter there.

The t-shirt came off first. The only thing between him and her now was a small scrap of lace. He had a fleeting thought as to whether she owned anything warmer when her exposed body made all thought flee.

"I'm going to make love to you, Taylor. I'm going to try and do it slow and easy. I want to savor you, taste you. I didn't wear protection before. I should have been more careful. But I'm clean and I know that you are. Will you let me know if...I'd like to know if there is a child, Taylor?"

"Yes. I'll tell you. I don't...I don't want children. I don't think I would...kiss me, Byron, please?"

He cupped her cheeks in both of his hands and kissed her again. He deepened the kiss even as his hand moved down her back to cup her firm ass and bring her closer to him. The counter was the perfect height for him; he only needed to lean down slightly to have her right where he wanted her. He pressed her back against the wood and leaned into her.

Her hands at his zipper made him pause and lean back a little. He watched as her hand disappeared into his pants and he closed his eyes when she wrapped her hand around him. Her grip was firm, but not like when they had played. This was more a caress. He couldn't stop himself from rocking into her fingers.

"I want to taste you. I loved the feeling of you in my mouth, deep in my throat. Will you let me suck your cock?"

She had already dropped her legs and was moving to her knees. He wanted to be inside of her, but the thought of feeling her lips over his cock again was all he could think about. When she pulled his jeans and boxers down to his knees and pressed him against the wall, he was beyond telling her no.

Taylor licked his tip first, taking the small drop of pearly cum into her mouth. Her moan nearly undid him and he gripped the counter for support. She looked up at him as she wrapped her lips over him and moved down over his shaft. He groaned. Nothing had ever felt that good. Her hands moved along his thighs and then along his ass. When she cupped him and pulled him closer to her mouth, he moved his free hand to her hair and moved it back so that he could see her face as she took him.

Her eyes were closed and she looked...beautiful seemed such a tame word for what she looked like to him. Her face was flushed and every time she dipped her head down on him, her eyes fluttered. He pumped into her heat and she moaned.

"Taylor, if you keep this up, I'm going to come down your throat. For as much as I'd love that, that's not where I want to come." She nipped his cock and squeezed tighter. He felt his eyes roll in the back of his head. Okay, he thought, just this once.

Her fingers moved along his balls and she rolled them in her palm. There was just enough pressure there to cause them to tighten closer to his body. He was rocking into her harder now and his grip on her hair was tight. There wasn't finesse now, only need, the need to come into her willing heat. When she slid her finger up his ass and teased his puckered hole, he lost it.

"Christ, Taylor, I'm coming."

He felt his cock jerk then his cum shoot into her. He was fucking her mouth hard and couldn't seem to slow down. Wave after wave emptied into her mouth. He felt her moan and swallow him. His entire body felt his climax, from the top of his head to the bottom of his feet. When he could take no more, he pulled her head back and her mouth left his now softening cock with a pop.

His breathing was sharp and ragged. His heart was pounding in his chest and he felt drained. She hadn't moved, but her head leaned against his thigh, as she, too, was breathing hard. Leaning down, he pulled her into his arms and sat her back on the counter. He kissed her.

Byron could taste himself on her; her tongue was salty from his cum and he felt his cock twitch again. She was going to kill him if she did that again. Then when she nipped at his nipple, he decided he didn't care.

He unsnapped her bra and as he tossed it to the floor with his discarded pants and her shirt, he took her nipple into his mouth. He loved the way it hardened in his mouth, the way it elongated and stiffened when he rolled it. He moved his hand beneath and lifted it up as he took more of it into his mouth. With his free hand, he worked her snap and zipper open. Reaching into her jeans, she felt the dampness of her panties.

"Help me get them off. I want you naked. Hurry." She shimmied out of her pants, but left her panties on. When she had laid back to remove them, he wouldn't let her up when he pulled them off her. "My turn. I'm going to feast on you." Pulling the stool closer, he sat and looked at the bounty before him.

Her panties were soaked and he moved the tiny scrap of material to the side as he put his hand on her knee to widen her for him. He slid his finger along her and then tasted the cream he had gathered. She tasted delicious.

"These have to go." He grabbed her panties and jerked them off her. Her breasts bounced with the force of his movement and he leaned forward, suckled just her nipple into his mouth, and worried it with his tongue ring. Kissing his way down her body, he nipped first then soothed the area with his tongue and kisses. She was panting by the time he was at her hips.

"Byron, you're driving me crazy. Please, stop teasing me and do it already."

He grinned up at her. "Do what? What is it you want me to do to you, love? This?" He slid one of his fingers into her heat, back and forth, fast for a few strokes then slower. "Or this?" He slid a second then a third finger into her.

"Yes. That's it! More, please, I want you to do it. Please, touch me." Her hips were coming up off the counter and he wanted to feel her surrounding him, but not yet. He wanted to, no, he needed to taste her.

"Say it, baby. Say what you want me to do to you, or I'll just keep teasing your pussy with my fingers and not anything else. Say what you want me to do to you."

"Lick me, taste me, please. Byron, I beg you. Please." He spread her nether lips open with his fingers, took her clit into his mouth, and nipped her.

He knew that she was close to coming, but she came apart immediately. Holding her legs open with his shoulders, he fucked her with his tongue as he lapped up her juices. She rode him, her hips surging up, her feet planted on the counter. His grip on her thighs held her steady as he continued to drink from her.

Her body was still trembling when she went limp in his arms. He didn't move from where he was, but watched her body, now sated, relaxed on the counter. When the tremors lessened, he picked her up in his arms and carried her up to his bed. His cock was hard again, but he wasn't sure either of them would survive if he took her again so soon.

He laid her on the bed and crawled in beside her. Taylor rolled over and wrapped her body over his and sat up to look at him when his cock nudged her thigh. Sliding her leg over his waist, she sat up on his hips.

"You want me again? I thought men could only come once or twice a week. Or is this because of something else?" Her smile was teasing.

"No, I want you again. But I'm willing to wait. You'll be sore. I wasn't very gentle with you your first time and you came three times downstairs."

"Five times. I want to feel you inside of me, Byron. Will it hurt you if I want you again?"

He reached over to his bedside table and tried to open the drawer while lying flat. She moved his hand and opened it for him. Reaching inside, she pulled out the box of condoms and looked at the box. Quirking a brow at him, she pulled one off the strip and opened it with her teeth.

"I don't know how to do this. Show me." She moved back to his thighs and watched as he rolled the latex over his engorged cock.

She ran her hand up and down him as he watched. She was like a small child in her curiosity, but all woman in her body. He stilled her hand with his.

"Sit up on your knees and come down slowly on my cock. Slowly, Taylor. You're not used to my size and I want you to enjoy this too." She did as he asked and he felt her body adjusting to his girth and length.

Christ, she was tight. When she was nearly halfway over him, he pulled her forward and kissed her. Taking her hips in his hands, he rocked her up and down his shaft as he stretched her and soon, she took him to the hilt. When she looked up at him, there were tears in her eyes. He didn't ask her. He thought he knew what she was feeling. At least, he hoped that she was.

Perfect. Their bodies fit perfectly. Rolling her to her back, she spread her legs and he settled between them. Looked down at her, her cheeks flushed, lips swollen from his kisses and his cock, her nipples hard against his chest and her heat wrapped around him, he knew that his mother was right. Rocking once into her, deep, he knew also that Taylor was his and that he was never letting her go. He had fallen in love with her sometime over the past month. And rather than feel overwhelmed by it, by all that it meant, he smiled. He had found his true love. Now he just needed to convince her of it.

Her climax was slow to build, as was his. This time, as he watched her, he saw the way her ears reddened at the tips and her

139

eyes darkened to the deepest blue. Her breath caught when he moved just right and her mouth opened when she was ready to moan. He loved the way her mouth felt against his and her tentative way of touching him, the way she got bolder as she grew closer. He nipped at her lower lip and suckled it into his mouth and marveled at her taste. When she peaked, she tightened her fingers into his arms and wrapped her feet around his calves. Throwing back her head, she bared her neck to him and he sank his teeth into the tender flesh, marking her with his mouth, marking her as his. Her body tightening around his brought him to his own release, hard and powerful. Mine, he though, she is all mine.

Byron rolled to his back, bringing her with him. She lay lax against him and when she snored softly, he moved out from under her to go to the bathroom and clean up. This time, when he looked in the mirror, he had the same thought. He was so fucked. Only this time, he was glad for it. Grabbing something from his dresser drawer, he crawled back into bed with her and was pleased when she rolled over him again. Smiling, Byron set his alarm and performed one more task. Within minutes, he was sound asleep.

~~~

"Wake up, damn it. Byron! The stupid alarm is going off. And I have to pee. Would you please un-cuff me? I cannot believe you actually put a pair of...wake up!"

She had been shaking him for the past ten minutes. She wouldn't admit it to him, but she had actually been quite pleased that he cuffed her. To her it meant that he didn't want her to leave. Crazy and stalker like, but she didn't care. She punched him hard in the arm again and squealed when he flipped her onto her back, his body pressing down on her.

"Stop hitting me. I'm not a morning person and I've not had my coffee. Unless you want to find it very difficult to sit today at work, I would suggest you give me three minutes of peace so that I can wake up at this ungodly hour. Who in their right mind gets up this early anyway and why?" He rolled over, taking her with him, and threw his arm over her waist.

There was no way she was going to laugh at him, but she found it incredibly funny that he needed peace and quiet. She enjoyed it too, but loved the morning hours. She watched his clock until five more minutes passed, then started to tickle his ribs. He growled at her and swatted her ass. It hurt like hell, but she needed him to get up.

"Please, at least un-cuff me. I have to get home and shower. I'm running out of time here and you still have to take me into work."

"Take my car. The keys are on the hanger by the door. No, take the SUV. It's better in the snow. You know how to drive, don't you? Good. Leave me your cell phone number and when the sun is straight up in the sky, I'll call you. Can I come in and have lunch with you?"

"Yes, I can drive, but I'm not taking your car. You just need to get up and take me home. Come on, Byron. Get up."

For an answer, he rolled over and pulled the covers over his head. Then suddenly, he pulled them down again and reached under his pillow to pull out the key to the cuffs. After unlocking them, he pulled her in for a deep, hot kiss then rolled over again.

"Leave me your cell number. I'll see you at lunch time."

She huffed out of the bed. "I'm going to total your car for this. I don't want to be responsible for your stuff. You said you'd take me in." If she had stomped her foot, it would have been a perfect demonstration of a snit, she thought.

"Total it, I don't care. It's insured. The only person that'll be pissed is Nicky. He thinks wrecking a car is paramount to robbing a bank. Go before you're late. I'll see you at lunch." He mumbled something else, but she was sure she had heard him wrong. Stomping down the stairs, she gathered up their clothes, pulled hers on, and put his on the washer. She went to his cabinet and pulled out a coffee thermos, filled it with the tea from the refrigerator, and went to the garage.

To say that this was a car was a complete understatement. It was more of a house on wheels. It was bigger than her room at the Y. Frowning and wondering if she should go back in and make sure one more time that he didn't want to take her himself, she opened it up and crawled in.

It took her two minutes to find the ignition, and several more to find how to turn the radio down. It had startled her so badly that she still had her hand over her heart when the engine turned over. The dash looked like what she thought a dash board on a plane must look like. Opening the garage door, she backed out of the darkened cavern and onto his street.

By the time she made it back to her room and cleaned up, she was nearly ten minutes behind. She had never driven anything so high off the road and was terrified of running up over a couple of smaller cars when she stopped at a light. She was glad for the dark window because no one could see how embarrassed she was. She pulled into the parking lot at twenty minutes after nine and nearly fell on her face getting out of the thing. She had never been so happy to see that she was the only one in the office and settled down to work.

There were three emails from the Freedoms, one from Jason and two from Paul. They were both saddened that she was leaving and wondered if there was anything they could do to convince her to stay. She was sure they wouldn't have anything she wanted and didn't answer. She thought she would work on a tactful letter later.

The second one from Paul was odd. It told her that she would be missed, much like his other letter, but his one was...well, creepier. He said how he had thought of her as someone he could trust and that he was slightly hurt that she could do this to them. It almost sounded as if he was accusing her of something and she wasn't sure of what it could be. She thought about it for a few more minutes and forwarded it to both Devin and Nickolas Grant. After she had sent it, she also forwarded it to Cait. She answered the other mail and then set about filing the payments in the ledger. Her cell phone ringing startled her.

"Hello, beautiful. Are you about ready for lunch? I was thinking a little taste of you with a quickie against the wall. Then maybe a little more of you for dessert."

"No, sorry, can't do it. I'm having lunch with an incredible lover, one that isn't too busy to get out of bed for me." Byron's laughter warmed her and settled over her like a comfortable blanket.

"Sorry, love, but I don't do mornings. You'd know this if you moved in here with me. Maybe next time you could persuade me to get up other ways. Riding my cock again could work."

She froze. Move in with him? Then she realized he was laughing and was glad that she hadn't said anything. Closing her eyes, she was thankful that she was leaving in three days. She didn't think her heart could take being around him.

"I can have lunch with you, but nothing more. I got here nearly thirty minutes late and I have to make up for the time or they'll dock me. Why don't we meet for dinner or something? Pizza sounds good." She realized she wanted to spend as much time as she could with him until she left.

"I'll cook you dinner. Come back here after work. If I'm not here for any reason, there's a house key on the ring you took. Let yourself in and wait for me, naked and in my bed preferably."

She told him she would and they hung up. The rest of the day was a blur; mostly because she kept catching herself at odd times thinking about what she thought he had said this morning before she left. There was no way he had said that he loved her.

Chapter Eighteen

Byron was still in the grocery store when Damon called. Margaret was in the hospital. She had slipped on the ice at work and may have broken her leg. Byron abandoned the cart and rushed to his car. He was nearly to the hospital when he called Taylor.

"My mom fell and I'm on my way to her. I don't know how long I'll be. Can you call me when you get off and I'll let you know how much longer I'll be?" He didn't want to break their date. He knew he had to talk to her.

"Oh, I hope she'll be all right. Don't worry about me. Just go to your mom. Okay, I'll go to your house, but you have to take me home. I'm not driving that thing again."

"We'll see. I'll call you as soon as I hear anything. Be careful." He was just pulling into the parking lot of the hospital when his brother called again. Damon was really good about keeping them informed.

"Mom's going to have to have surgery. The break wasn't clean and the surgeon is a little concerned about it. Mom's having a hissy fit, yelling at him because he wants her to stay until the day after Christmas. I'm betting she wins. Want to take odds?"

"No. One, because I agree, she'll be home before Christmas, and two, you'll make sure she is. I'm inside the hospital now. I'll be there in about three seconds."

He flipped his phone closed just as Damon stepped out from behind the curtain to his mom's area. Damon looked like hell and he was surprised by that. He started to ask when he heard his mother moan again.

"She's in a lot of pain and the fucking doctor won't give her anything. I'm going to sue his ass as soon as this is over. What the hell is taking so long? She should have been in surgery an hour ago."

"Damon, please sit down, you're making me nuts. Byr, please tell your brother to sit down. He's been pacing for twenty minutes." Bryon leaned over and kissed Cait's cheek as she started ordering everyone around. He loved the women of his family. He walked over to the bed and looked at his mom.

His mom looked...well, she looked old. He'd never noticed how much she had aged since he was a kid. Her hair was a nice shade of warm cocoa, but even though he would never ask her, he was sure it came from a salon and not her natural color — she was in her mid-sixties.

"Did you talk to Taylor? Did you figure things out? I'd like to know before they put me under the knife that you're not as stupid as your brothers think you are."

"Thanks, Mom, I'm glad you're in my corner. Figure out what? Oh! You mean that I love her? Then yes, I figured it out. I told her, but not properly. I was going to beg her to marry me tonight, but someone had to take a shortcut off the stairs and I'm here instead of with her. Your timing could be a little better, you know." He kissed her on the cheek and smoothed her hair from her forehead.

"You always were an ungrateful child. I should have beaten your bottom more instead of letting you convince me you were innocent. I knew better, but you could be quite persuasive when you wanted to be. Now, be a good boy and take Damon to the cafeteria and get him some coffee, or at least some chocolate. The man is driving me crazy. And call Taylor and tell her to get her ass over here right now. When I suffer, I want everyone to do it as well."

The surgeon came in just then with a nurse. The nurse hung a large bag of fluids on the long steel arm near the bed and then put a lead into his mom's hand. It always made him sort of dizzy to watch someone get stuck. It was doubly so with his mom. When the IV was in, the nurse pulled a needle out and started to push something into the site.

"This will make you drowsy, Mrs. Parker, and really relaxed. We aren't going to have you under long, but the doctor wants to make sure you're comfortable during the procedure."

Byron noticed his mom's face relaxing first then her eyes started to flutter closed. She was fighting it, but knew that she was trying to win an impossible battle. It wasn't long before she was relaxed enough that she was snoring. He smiled. Who knew she snored?

The surgery only lasted an hour. They had to set her leg with a pin to make it sturdy. She would be in a great deal of pain, but Damon had arranged to have her home on Christmas morning if things went well. He had already hired a nurse to stay with her and he would be moving in until she was better. Everyone seemed satisfied with the arrangement, especially Dan, their step-dad, who was at his wits end.

Byron had called Taylor twice and both times she'd made him smile. They hadn't talked about anything, but it just felt too good speaking to her. She couldn't come to the hospital until after five o'clock and Byron was sure by then they'd all be gone.

"Does she need anything? I can bring her something on my way home. I live right on the way past the hospital."

"No, she'll be sleeping until morning and you aren't going back to that place. I thought you said you were coming home with me? I'm going to go pick up a few things for dinner then I'll be at my house. You'll come there. I have a night of fun planned for you and you owe me."

"How do you figure I owe you? You made me drive that monstrosity to work after telling me that you'd take me. I didn't even have anything to wear once you tore things from my poor, abused body. Do you have any idea how much I paid for that little bra and panty set? And I'm not rich like some people I know."

"Come home with me and I'll buy you two sets of those sexy little things. And if you let me rip them from your body, I'll buy you four sets. Please? I have toys that I want to play with you with. I want to pink up your ass so beautifully that I may have to pay homage to it all night before I'm finished. Then I want to take your nipples and clamp them tight and watch them redden from it. Christ, woman, I'm so hard right now, I can't even go in the store to pick us up dinner." He thought about just going home and jerking off, but wanted to cook for her and he wasn't going to come without her. His cock would just have to wait, damn it. When she answered him, he nearly changed his mind and went home anyway.

"You make me wet with just your voice, did you know that? I've not been able to get a damned thing done today for thinking about what you did to me last night and how wet my panties are. I'll come to your house, but if you don't fuck me the second I walk in the door, I may have to hurt you."

He couldn't answer her at first. His throat had dried up and his tongue was stuck to the roof of his mouth. It was everything he could do to guide his car to the side of the road before he wrecked. He leaned his head on the steering wheel and took several deep breaths before he could speak.

"Come to my house naked under your coat. I don't care if you have to strip in the car in the driveway. You'd better have nothing on save those fuck me boots and a coat when I open the door. Do you understand me, Taylor? If you're not, I'm going to punish you in ways you've never thought of." He was panting and suddenly realized he could hear her doing the same.

"Yes, master. Naked except for my boots and coat when you open the door. And Byron, you'd better be ready or, so help me, you'll be punished in ways you've never heard of."

The phone went dead in his hand. Carefully, so that he didn't hurt himself or his car, he laid his phone on the passenger seat and sat there waiting for the roaring in his head to slow down. Christ, he was never going to make it until six o'clock.

~~~

At four-thirty, Taylor was pacing the office. Her body was a hum of live wires. Every nerve ending in her body, even at her toes, was making her skin feel like it didn't fit her. Her nipples hurt, not just ached, but hurt, and she wanted to take her bra off and rub them. Her panties had come off an hour ago and she knew that she was soaking the tops of her thighs; the cream was tickling as it dripped from her. Even her lips felt fuller and needier because of Byron. If he didn't hold on his promise, she would hurt him. Then rape him.

She had her coat on and her bag in her hand at three minutes until five o'clock and when the hand was straight up on the twelve, she was locking the door. Shaking her need for him so overwhelming, she had to stop and close her eyes with her head leaned back against the seat. It wouldn't do to kill herself before she got there. After several seconds of trying to relax, the key fit in the tiny slot and the engine turned over. Taylor drove extra slow to her place, making sure she concentrated on everything she did. When she pulled up, she hurried inside to get her things she would be taking with her to Florida and a set of clothes for her last day at work. She had purchased her ticket that afternoon before talking to Byron and she was nearly all set.

Driving to his house, she thought about the man she was going to sleep with. Well, sleep with was a stupid term because she knew there would be very little of actual sleeping unless one or both of them passed out. She was giddy with need for him and planned to get as much as she could from tonight. Byron Grant was a great lover and she was glad he had been her first.

He made her feel special and needed. The way he touched her sometimes made her want to crawl up in his lap and just have him hold her. She'd never wanted that before, not in all the time she'd been out on her own. She would miss him. Miss him much more than she was comfortable with.

Taylor had wondered about what she'd thought he said this morning. She thought he'd said he loved her. The flutter in her heart made her frown. Men were always saying that to women, she knew that. They'd say anything to get laid, she also knew that. But it hadn't felt like that when he'd said it. Even though it was muffled beneath the blankets, she felt the sincerity of his words.

But men like Byron didn't have to say they loved you to get into your pants; they just had to ask. Men like Byron also didn't fall in love with people like her, someone who had nothing and came from nothing. His type of man fell in love and married people like princesses and movie stars, women with pedigrees as long as your arm and money to back it up. Not a woman who could barely pay her rent and had to sell her car to buy plane tickets. By the time she pulled into his driveway, her mood had plummeted and it was all she could do to strip down in the huge car and put her coat back on. Wiping away the tears that had fallen at some point on the drive over, she decided that she was going to enjoy her last night with him and then in the morning when he dropped her off to work, she was going to spend the day thinking about him and then catch her plane at ten-thirty and never look back.

Sure, she was. And donkeys would fly too. Taylor had done something really stupid; she'd fallen in love with the arrogant ass.

Chapter Nineteen

Byron heard her pull into the drive and looked out. He wanted to run out and drag her in, but knew that he couldn't do that, at least not yet. He ached to be with her, to touch her, and he wanted her in ways he'd never wanted anyone before. He was startled when his cell phone rang.

"Are you all right? Why aren't you coming in?" he asked, and went to the window again. The engine was running and he was afraid she would leave.

"I want to cash in my freebie, the one from the other night. I'm in charge right now and you'll do what I say. All right?" He grinned and nodded then realized she couldn't see him.

"Yes. For now, you can be in charge. What do you want, Taylor? Come inside and tell me." His voice had gotten husky and his cock twitched in his jeans.

"Naked. I want you naked and ready for me. I'm going to take your cock into my mouth and I'm going to go down on you. I'm going to run my tongue along your length and nip at your pulse at the base. I want to feel the silky heat of you fill my mouth. My tongue is going to tease your slit and suckle at the cum that is gathering there right now. It is, isn't it, Byron, your cock is leaking for me?"

"Yes. I'm harder than I've ever been in my life. Come inside, Taylor. Do those things to me, please?"

"You'll not touch me. If you do then I'll stop. You don't want me to stop, not when I plan to take you deep into my throat, not when I want to wrap my tongue around your sac and pull your balls into my mouth and suck them, do you?"

"Christ! You're killing me. No. No, I don't want you to stop. I won't touch you. Are you wet, Taylor? Are you soaking my car seat with your juices?" He needed to get control of this, of her, before he did something incredibly stupid like beg, beg her like a Sub.

"I'm very wet. My pussy has been gushing all day since you called me. But you'll behave or you'll never feel me using my cream to lube up your ass and fuck you with my finger. You'll never feel me take you so far down my throat that when I swallow, you'll feel it tighten around you cock so hard you'll beg me to let you come. You want that, Byron? You want me to suck you that hard until you come?"

"Yes, master." His head was spinning. In that moment, he would gladly let the world know she was in charge. Relinquishing control to her made him harder, impossibly harder than he'd ever been.

"Good boy. Now, get your clothes off and be lean against the wall when I come inside. I'm going to take you as soon as the door is shut and you'd better be ready." The phone went dead and he closed his eyes. Then they popped back open when he heard the engine to the car shut off. In record time, he was stripped of his clothing and was turning off his phone when the knob of the door turned.

Her coat slipped off as she dropped a bag to the floor and her glorious body was exposed to him. He groaned, he couldn't help it, and when she dropped before him and licked his cock, he closed his eyes and leaned back against the wall for support.

~~~

Taylor reached between Byron's legs and fondled his balls gently. They were hot and hard, their weight felt good in her hands, and she licked them before wrapping her mouth over the crown of his cock. He surged forward and she saw his hands move then he pressed them behind him.

"Good. Now I'm going to play for a while and I don't want you to come just yet. I want to taste you fully before I let you slide down my throat and shoot all this delicious cream inside of me. Don't touch me or I will stop. If you try to take control again, I'll stop. Understand me, slave?"

She was afraid he would say no, afraid that he would know that she had never done anything like this before and was both terrified and excited to do this to him and for him. She looked up when he didn't answer right away and nearly came apart. Lust and need filled his eyes, his breathing was fast, and she could see his pulse pound at his throat.

"Yes, master. I understand. I...Christ, you're beautiful. I'll behave." Her heart fluttered in her chest and she closed her eyes before he could read the love in hers.

Running her tongue up the heavy, pulsing vein, she nipped at the tight skin there. She ran her fingers along his thighs and circled them around to cup his ass and pull him forward. Closing her mind to him, she set to work memorizing every inch of him, his textures, and his smell. She loved the way he filled her mouth when she took him in, the taste of his pre-cum when he leaked at the tip. His balls tightened against his body and she could feel the way they moved heavily within their tight sac. Lost in her own world of loving him, she nearly missed the way his legs were trembling and she looked up at him.

His face was tight; the cords of muscle at his neck were strained and pronounced. His mouth was pressed tight together and she could see the pain there. He was holding back, controlling his climax as she had told him to do.

"Would you like to come now, slave? Come down my throat?"

His hiss of "yes" raced along her skin like hot lava. The look in his eyes promised payback and need. Her pussy gushed more and she could feel her own climax racing along her never endings. As he watched her, she put her fingers into her pussy and she coated him with her juices. Running a bit of it along his crown to coat him, she then licked him clean. His answering growl made her see stars.

Coating her fingers again, this time, she moved them along his ass cheeks and then along the seam. His surge into her mouth she took as his approval. Coating the puckered hole, she looked up at him and waited.

"Do it, do it now," he begged, and she took him deep in her throat and, like she promised, swallowed him at the same time she punched her finger through the tight ring of muscles in his ass.

KATHI S. BARTON

He came hard; the first jet of cum that hit the back of her throat was hot and heavy. She never gagged like she had before but swallowed again and again, taking him deeper and deeper into her. When his hand cupped the back of her head and he began fucking her hard with his cock, she didn't care. He was coming inside of her. Over and over he released in her and with every forward surge of his hips, she moved inside of his hot ass. When he was empty and slumped against the wall, Taylor let go of his cock, slid her hands down to her lap, laid her head on his thigh and tried to regain control of her body. Tremors racked her and she needed relief badly, but she was fine — for now.

It wasn't until Byron picked her up that she realized she had fallen asleep. Her body hummed with need, but she also felt more relaxed than she had in months. She cuddled tight against his neck and nipped at his shoulder.

"Did you enjoy that, Byron? It was all right, wasn't it?" She yawned hugely and snuggled deeper.

"You need to ask? Christ, woman, I thought you'd forgotten me you were enjoying yourself so much. It was well worth it. The look on your face, the way you...everything about it was...yes, love, it was more than all right." She felt the bed beneath her. He must have taken her to his room.

"You cheated. You touched me. I'll have to do it again until you learn to behave," she said as she drifted off to sleep.

Taylor came awake screaming. The climax was so hard and so unexpected she sat up and tried to pull away from the overwhelming sensations. Byron didn't stop, though; he lapped at her clit over and over while wave after wave of aftershocks rippled through her.

"Please, please, you have to stop, I can't...it's too much." He just looked up at her, grinned, and buried his face back between her legs.

Using his shoulders, he opened her legs wider and then cupped her ass to bring her more firmly to his mouth. He was watching her now. She could feel his eyes on her as she came down from her climax by degrees. The ring in his tongue was pressed hard against her clit and he rubbed it to and fro until she could feel the heat building again.

"Squeeze your breasts for me and roll those luscious nipples. Make them stand up hard for me, Taylor." His voice, the one that shimmered over her like a silken sheet, made her need to do what he wanted. Lying back on the bed, she did what he asked as he took her higher and higher again.

He had a wicked tongue and the ring on the tip could roll along her in ways she'd never dreamed of. When he spread her wider with his thumbs at the mouth of her opening, she wrapped her thighs around his neck and tried to hold him closer. She could feel his chuckle against her leg.

"Please, master, I need to come again. Please?" And she did. He hadn't given her time to pace herself or force her body to obey him and she was spiraling closer to a hard release quicker than she'd ever been able to before.

"When we're in this bed, we aren't playing, Ta. When we play, it'll be in the playroom and you'll know. Right now, we are two people making love and enjoying each other's bodies, understand? If you want to come, then by all means, let it go. I love watching you come and when you do it with my mouth over you, you fill me with such delicious cream. Come, sweetheart, come for me again."

This climax rolled through her, not hard, not even quick, but like a slow moving army. Conquering one area to the point of complete triumph before moving on, taking no prisoners on the way. Starting at her head, it moved along her brain and made her seize up; thought, breathing, even heartbeat seemed to stop for several seconds while the climax took control. By the time it made it to her nipples, they were swollen and hard, achy to feel something, someone suckle at them. When Byron pushed two then three fingers deep into her, she peaked again, harder and longer before the first one was complete. Just when she was coming down off one, he would bring another fast on its heels until she begged him to stop, begged him please no more.

He slid up her body then and kissed her, devoured her mouth as his cock nudged at her opening. His plea of, "let me in" had her spreading wide and unbelievably ready for him to bring her again. His cock stretched her, opened her, and filled her. His strokes were strong and true, hitting her perfectly inside and bringing her, both of them, to what she realized was going to be the best orgasm

155

either of them had ever had. When he roared out his release, surging hard into her, spilling into her, she came with him, screaming out his name as loudly as he did hers. Falling into an exhausted sleep, she smiled knowing that she loved this man and would for the rest of her life.

"Wake up. Come on, Taylor, wake up or I'll feed you your steak raw and your baked potato covered in bacon." She didn't want to wake up. She was sated and warm. Snuggling deeper into the covers, she was surprised when they were jerked away and a hand came down hard on her ass.

"Hey! That fucking hurt. Go away. I'm tired. It's the middle of the flipping night. Aren't you tired?" She could smell it then, food. And her belly made an answering call. She looked up at Byron, alarmed.

"See, you need food. And it is the middle of the night. It's my time of the day. Now you have thirty seconds to get up and pull on something to cover that delectable body or I'm coming in here and making love to you again. And this time, I won't be easy."

She looked at him with raised brows. That was supposed to be a threat? Not likely. She grinned and cupped her breasts while she licked her lips. The seduction might have been better if her belly hadn't decided to growl again, louder and longer than before. Byron was laughing when he left the room, shouting "twenty-five seconds" over his shoulder.

Taylor really was hungry and jumped up to pull on something when she saw his shirt. Her panties were still in her bag in the kitchen, so she was buttoning the last button on his shirt when she entered the kitchen.

"Good, five seconds left. How do you want your steak? I also have fries if you'd rather have those. I realized when I was turning on the grill we've never had dinner together. After Christmas, we'll take care of that."

"Fries, and I don't eat steak. I don't care for red meat." The look on his face was priceless and she couldn't help but continue teasing him. "You don't eat red meat, do you? Omigod! I can't see anyone that consumes beef. You'll have to take me home and oof! Let me go, you idiot." He had grabbed her around the waist and pulled her into his lap. She knew he was going to swat her and tensed for the contact. It didn't come, but the caress did. And oh, what a caress it was.

"Not eat red meat indeed. You scared the shit out of me. For that, you get yours well done. Ummm, you have the most beautiful ass. Has anyone ever said that to you? I could nibble on it all night. But for now." He stood dropping her to the floor. "I'll have a steak with fries. You?"

"Fries. And rare on the steak. You make it well and I'll strangle you with it. Do you have barbeque sauce? And what kind of veggies do you have?"

"You are not putting barbeque sauce on your steak. I will not let you ruin a perfectly good cut of meat with sauce. And no veggies, my house, my rules. Just don't tell my mother."

"Not for the steak, you moron, for the fries. And you should eat veggies at least once a day. They'll keep you heal—"

"I'd rather eat you. In fact, you can be my appetizer." He picked her up, sat her on the counter, and stepped between her legs. "I can't believe the incredible climax I had with you not two hours ago and I want you again. You're going to kill me, woman."

She didn't know how far they would have gone if the timer hadn't gone off. Her heart was pounding in her chest and she was wet again. It was a good thing she was leaving after tonight; they'd probably kill one another within a week if they lived together.

Then she remembered that she was leaving. This time tomorrow night, she'd be looking for a place to sleep. In Florida, not Ohio.

Chapter Twenty

Byron knew something had changed when he turned back to her from the oven. Taylor looked like she wanted to cry and the sadness in her eyes was profound. He wondered what he had said or done.

"Baby, it'll be okay. I was only kidding. Not about my mom knowing about the veggies, because she will kill me, but about the steak. I'll make it rare for you."

"No, it's nothing. I was just thinking about how I have to work tomorrow, that's all. I really hate my job. I'm going to get another one soon and I'll be all right."

He knew that wasn't it, but he let it go, for now. When they sat down to steak and fries and warm rolls, they ate like they'd been starved. He supposed they had been. He knew he'd not had anything to eat since he'd had a quick burger at around noon yesterday and they had both used up a great deal of energy since she'd come over. He hoped to expend a great deal more.

"Are you going to go work for Devin and Nick? They'll be good to work for. Nicky can be a bit stiff at times and since Ronnie, Devin is a little distracted, but they'll treat you right. I know they were both impressed with your skills the day Donna left."

"No, I can't work for them. I don't think I would make it a week without killing one or both of them. And calling Nick stiff is a bit of an understatement, wouldn't you say? Nah, I'll find a good job this time."

Dinner was over and they were cleaning up when he noticed that she was yawning again. He then realized that she'd been up since she left his house yesterday morning, while he had slept until almost one. As much as he wanted to make love to her again, he knew that she was exhausted.

"Come on, sweetie, let's get you to bed. You've had a long day and you have to get up in four hours to do it all again. I didn't realize it was so late. Why don't you call off. I can't believe their making you work on Christmas Eve. Don't they have a heart?" He watched the pained look streak across her face. Had he not been looking at her, he would have missed it.

"Jamie said the same thing at Thanksgiving. I am tired. Are you coming to bed with me? You're very snuggly." When she leaned in for a kiss, he swatted her ass.

"I am not now nor have I ever been snuggly. And yes, I'll come to bed with you, but no sex. You're probably very sore and I don't want to hurt you. Tomorrow night, we play." Throwing her over his shoulder, he took her to bed and dropped her on it. "Behave, or I'll tie you down."

He wanted to take her again, but the look was there again. She looked so sad, and he didn't know what do to about it. Byron was going to have to talk with Jamie. He knew that's what was making her sad and he would make them talk it out. Tomorrow night they'd all be at his mother's and he'd get them together then. Closing his eyes, thinking he'd just take a short nap and then go out and work, he fell asleep with Taylor snoring gently across his chest.

Byron woke to Taylor riding his cock. She was riding him hard and her pace was quick. Looking at her she, was cupping her breasts and her head was thrown back. She looked like a goddess. His moan made her aware of him and she looked at him with glazed eyes.

"You feel so good like this. I'm so full with you this deep. Please, help me come, Byron. I need to come in the worst way." Her thighs were locked tight against his and her rhythm was becoming erratic and her moans longer and louder. He wondered how long she'd been up and realized it had been long enough that she looked ready to come.

"Lick your nipples for me, baby. I want you to take those hard peaks into your mouth and suckle them like I do. That's it. Oh,

Taylor, you are a vision to behold riding me this way. I want to shoot my come into right now, like this."

"Please, now. I'm so close, I'm...Byron! I'm coming!" Her legs tightened over him and her body bowed. Grabbing her hips tight, he surged into her and felt her sheath grip him tight, rippling along his cock so hard it felt like she was going to pinch him off at the root. Waiting until she was coming down, he flipped her to her back and surged hard once, twice and then once more before he was roaring into her again, her body coming again around him.

He collapsed on her and couldn't move. He was dead, he just knew it. As soon as his heart started to maintain a normal beat and his breathing was under some control, he rolled to his back taking Taylor with him.

"I never thought I'd say this and I'll deny it if asked, but no more. I'm done in. If you want to make love again, I swear to you I don't think I can do it. Please, let me rest. Go to sleep." Her giggle made him smile and it was the last thing he remembered as he slipped into a sated slumber.

~~~

As soon as she knew he was asleep, Taylor slipped from his bed. Her body hurt and ached in more places than she knew she had, but she needed him to sleep past the time she left. Standing over his bed looking down at him, she knew that he'd be the only man she'd ever love.

Going to the bathroom, she took a quick shower and dressed. At some time through the night he must have brought her bag up. Ten minutes after leaving his bed, Taylor was making her way to the kitchen. Sitting at the table, she pulled out the notes she had written at work, one for Jamie and the other for Byron. She opened Jamie's first.

"Jamie,

I'm sorry to have disappointed you. I never meant to. You have been and always will be my friend. Know that please.

I got you this gift for your promotion. I remembered you telling me that once you were tenured you were going to buy you some so I did it for you. I don't know if you'll wear them or not, but I wanted you to have them all the same.

161

You have a good life. I'll miss you terribly and if you're ever in Florida, don't look me up. LMFAO. No, I don't know where I'll end up, but that is where I belong. You take care.

Love you very much, Taylor"

She folded it up and returned it to its envelope. Next, she took out the one for Byron. It had been incredibly hard to write, but she was sure he'd get over her soon enough. She laid it down and called the cab before pulling it out to re-read.

"Byron,

These past few weeks with you were wonderful. You showed me so much in so little time that I'm not sure I'll ever be the same again.

I'm not stealing away in the middle of the night this time, but leaving because I have to. I will miss you and think about you often.

Be good to yourself. I wish you a long and happy life. Good-bye, I love you.

Taylor

P.S. Could you please see that Jamie gets this box and the other envelope? Don't tell him it's from me."

Nearly sobbing, she folded the letter and stuck in back in the envelope. She was just sticking them both and the small box in his coat pocket when she heard the taxi pull up. She hurried and grabbed her things and left before she could change her mind. It was the hardest thing she'd ever done.

Taylor was only going to work half a day. Her plane took off at ten-thirty tonight and she had to be at the airport by nine. There wasn't anyone she wanted to say good-bye too other than her few friends she had met at the campus and no one who would be overly sad that she didn't tell them of her plans. At ten in the morning, the cell phone rang. Making a mental note to make sure she left it for Devin, she answered it.

"Taylor Bennett." Closing her eyes, she wished she had remembered to look at the caller ID before she answered. But she was surprised to hear Cait's voice.

"Hello. I just got your email from Paul Freedom. Did you send it to Nick or Devin? It's a strange note, don't you think?"

"Yeah, I sent it to both of them. It came with another one too, one that said he was sorry I was leaving, but not like this one. Jason sent one too, but another sorry and can we give you something to stay sort of stuff."

"Devin said he offered you a job, are you going to take it? You couldn't do better working for them. They may be a bit to take at times, but they are loyal to those they deem friends."

"First of all, I doubt either of them thinks of me as a friend. Secondly, no, I'm not. I told you I was leaving. Why is that so hard for anyone to remember?"

Taylor heard a car pull in the parking lot and didn't know who it was. The car had the name of a rental place on it, but she couldn't see who was in it. Oh well, probably just doing some last minute shopping.

"Does Byron know you're leaving? Have you told him that you love him yet? He's not going to just let you go, you know. I think he genuinely cares for you, Taylor. Maybe even loves you."

"Sure he does. And my Aunt Isadora was a saint. Yes, I told him. Sort of, anyway. What difference does it make? And I don't love him." She looked up in time to see Paul Freedom get out of the car and she swore he had a gun. "Shit! You guys have me so worked up about this insurance thingy that I'm seeing things. Damn it, why did you have to say they'd kill me?"

"Tell me what has you spooked, Taylor. Right now, tell me." Taylor heard the panic in the other woman's voice and reacted to it.

"Paul Freedom, he's getting out of a rental car and I think I saw a gun. He's coming in. See what you've done?"

"Taylor, is there a back door to the place? Somewhere you can hide until I can get a unit over there?" Panic made Taylor's mind shut down. He would be in the building any minute and there was a gun.

"No. He has a gun. One in his hand. I...he'll be here any minute. Oh, Christ, he's going to kill me, isn't he? I'm so sorry. Tell—"

"Listen to me! Lay the phone down, but don't let him see it. I want to hear everything he says. Be calm. I'm sending a unit to you now. Taylor, keep him talking."

She laid the phone on the desk and covered it with a tissue. Taylor was trembling so hard she wasn't sure how she would keep him from noticing and picked up her bag and began searching through it as if looking for something. She was frowning, thinking of what to say, when he opened the door.

"Well, hello, Taylor. I didn't know if you'd show up today. It being your last day and all." She looked up, surprised that he sounded so normal when everything inside of her was jumping like a kid high on sugar.

"I told you I'd be in today, Mr. Freedom. I've never lied to you. I don't suppose you brought me my last paycheck, did you? I sure could use it." She tried to giggle, but it came off sounding manic even to her.

"Hummm, no. Are you alone here? Any clients come in? I thought I heard you talking to someone." She watched as he went to the two offices and tested the doors. Both were locked and she didn't have a key.

"Singing. I was singing Christmas carols. You know, trying to get into the spirit of things. You going anywhere for Christmas, Mr. Freedom?"

"You know, Taylor, if you would have just waited until March, none of this would have been necessary. We needed that extra time to get the money transferred and laundered, but you leaving now, well, it put a damper on things for us."

"I'm afraid I don't know what you're talking about. What wouldn't have been necessary? And what money?" She was terrified. Taylor could feel the sweat trickle down her spine.

"The insurance money. We thought you'd be too stupid to figure it out, and it turns out, we were correct. Hire stupid, Jason said. Too bad he had to die too. We might have been able to pull this little scam somewhere else with his help. But it couldn't be helped. He wanted to back out and come clean. The stupid bastard actually came to like you"

"Jason is dead? What happened to him?" If a man could kill his own brother, then he really wouldn't have any trouble killing her.

"You killed him. Well, that's what the police are going to think. A jealous rage, I think it looks like. He and his girlfriend are going to be found dead in their bed and you are going to be blamed. I've been setting that up for weeks, little notes to his email address from you. Little notes hidden in his office. Yes, ma'am, some days it was just too much fun making you two pretend lovers. You're also going to be blamed for the missing money. It's all in your name."

"I didn't take any money, you did. You were collecting from dead—" Shit!

"Ah, so you did figure it out, did you? Oh well, it's too late now. Yes, collecting money from the dead. You didn't file the correct paperwork and took that money for yourself. Bad girl, you should have to go to jail, but I have better plans. Come on now, gather your things and get in the car. We're going for a ride, you and me."

She wanted to giggle because she thought about all those flipping movies she'd been watching since she'd found the money and it was all true. She was going to die because she had stuck her nose where it didn't belong.

"I don't want to die, Mr. Freedom. I won't tell anyone, I promise. I was going to Florida tonight and no one will ever know." The slap came fast and it knocked her to the floor.

"Get out there now, bitch. I don't have time for this shit. Grab your stuff and get going." Spittle came from his mouth and she thought there was foam there. Hysterics were making her giggle and he slapped her again.

Grabbing up everything off the desk, she dumped it in her purse and hoped that Cait was sending someone to rescue her. But she happened to glance at the phone and saw the low battery warning and almost cried. It would be dead soon. She'd never charged it in all the time she'd had it.

She was shoved in the front seat of the car and he dumped her things in the seat beside her. Holding the gun on her as he moved around the front of the car, he got in the driver's door and put on his seat belt. His mumbled "seat belt" had her giggling again and it earned her a cuff to the face. If he kept this up, she'd be dead before they got out of the parking lot. When they were about three blocks from the office, three cruisers sped past them in the opposite direction. Too late.

KATHI S. BARTON

Chapter Twenty-One

The pounding was reverberating through his head. Byron never answered the door before noon and whoever it was at his door was going to pay for this. He nearly went naked, but at the last minute grabbed his jeans and slipped them on without bothering to snap them. Jerking open the door nearly had him slamming it shut again on who was standing there. Spencer was a dead man.

"This had better be fucking important or Cait will be a widow before your kid is born. What the fuck do you want?"

"Taylor's been kidnapped. Get dressed. I'll take you to the house. Mom said not to let you drive. O'Malley has been trying to reach you for an hour."

Byron only moved to drop to the floor. Everything in the room kept spinning around and every time he thought he had a handle on it, it was spinning again. He felt Spencer push his head between his knees and talk to him.

"Come on; don't fall apart on me now. I need you to get dressed so we can help find her. Please, Byr, get it together. We'll find her and bring her back."

"I'm okay. I'm going to be okay. I have to...what happened? She was here until...she had to work today and must have...my car, does she have it? We can track her with the GPS."

"No. There were no cars in the lot when the police got there. Taylor told O'Malley that Paul Freedom had a rental. He came in the office and held her at gun point and she left with him. That girl of yours, she's a smart cookie. O'Malley said she remained calm the whole time he was telling her what he was going to do to her."

"I'll give her an award when I see her again," Byron snarled at his brother. "Damn it, Spence, I love her. Did he hurt her? If he did, I'm going to kill him."

"O'Malley thinks he hit her a couple of times. The police tracked them as far as they could before the battery on her phone died. The Feds are taking over the case and their toys are better than the locals. Byron, come on, we need to get going. Mom is beside herself with worry and needs to see you. She's terrified we aren't telling her something and she's afraid you're hurt too."

Spencer's phone was ringing and as he answered it, Byron made himself get up and get moving. He had to take a quick shower to wash away some of the sleep still lingering in his body and was getting dressed when he thought of a few things to ask Spencer. He stepped into his room and his brother was there, along with Jamie.

"Have you heard anything yet? Do you know what time he took her? How long she's been...gone?" He couldn't say kidnapped. That sounded so final and he wasn't going there. He glanced at Jamie. He looked devastated.

"Around ten-thirty or so. Taylor was on the phone with O'Malley when he came in and she had Taylor lay the phone on the desk so she could hear. There's something else that's not known by the media yet. Paul apparently killed his brother Jason and a girl he was seeing. It was brutal and savage. He'd been setting Taylor up for months now, leaving notes from her to Jason, emails and stuff. I just found out that the accounts had been in Taylor's name for over a year. Taylor figured it out around Thanksgiving and has been working with Devin since the night Marie was born. I don't know the exact figure, but it's right around seven hundred million in insurance fraud."

"And now kidnapping and murder. Christ, if I had let her stay with me, she'd be safe right now. This is my fault." Jamie crumbled to the chair and started sobbing.

"She's been staying here, Jamie, and it didn't matter. Taylor has been with me for the past three nights and I couldn't keep her safe. He was a fool to mess with ours. He'll make a mistake and we'll get him and bring her home. I swear. I love her and I need her. Please don't blame yourself. She'll kick your ass if she hears about it and you know it." Byron got what he hoped for, a little chuckle from Jamie.

He was pulling his coat on when the envelopes fell out. The small box nearly hit the floor, but Jamie was close enough to snag it before it did. He handed it to back and Byron handed him the envelope with his name on it.

"This is for you." Byron watched as his brother opened it up and when he had apparently read it, he dropped to the chair right behind him. Spencer handed Jamie a glass of water.

"The box, it's from Taylor. She...Christ, she bought it for me. It's the cufflinks, I'm betting. I've been coveting them for years. She must have...she bought them for me and I treated her like shit. Byr, what have I done?"

"We'll get her back. We have to, now buck up. Mom will be pissed enough that she's gone. Let's not give her any reason to be more pissed off. Byron, get in that monster you call a car. Jamie, open your gift or not, but let's get a move on." Both Byron and Jamie looked at each other then their brother.

"You keep that up and I'm telling Cait what you got her for Christmas. You so won't be a happy man if I do that to you," Byron teased.

"You wouldn't...yes, you would. All right, but we do need to get moving. I'll drive. I promised Mom I would and I don't know about you, but I'd rather have fifty women like O'Malley mad at me than my mom right now."

They went by the hospital first to see their mother. She asked to talk to Byron alone and the others walked out. Damon was still seeing patients so he wouldn't be in until later.

"There's something I need to tell you. Something you should know. It's about Taylor. She...well, she's a submissive. I don't know what you can do to help her, but you should know." Byron looked at his mother for a whole ten seconds and threw back his head and laughed. He kissed her on her mouth and then on her forehead.

"How long have you known? I should have known better than to try and keep things from you. What else? I suppose you know about the clubs too. Dam...err, darn it, Mom, what am I going to do with you? I won't hurt her."

"Good heavens, Byron, I know that. And I've known since you bought the first shop. The property you bought, didn't you think the price was a little cheap, even for that size of a building?"

"You owned the building. I'll be damned. You sneaky little...did you tell Dan? Of course you did. 'Never keep a secret from a spouse.' I'm going to marry her when I find her, because we will. I plan to make her very happy. And I also thought you should know I need her. Need her with a passion I've never felt for anyone other than you. I love you, Mom."

"I know you do, son. I need you too. Now get out of here and find that girl. That bastard fucked with the wrong family when he took someone we love." Byron wasn't sure if he was shocked more by the passion in her voice or the words that accompanied it. Kissing her again, he decided that he would just keep that to himself.

He pulled out the envelope when they got back in the car and he decided he wasn't reading it. He opened the glove box and shoved it in there with the other things he wanted to forget, mostly parking tickets. The police station was a hive of activity when they arrived.

~~~

Taylor felt the cold air surrounding her. She wanted to snuggle closer to Byron, but she couldn't move. Then the pain rippled through her, jerking her awake. The gag in her mouth kept her from screaming.

"Ah yes, there you are. You've been out so long that I didn't think I'd get to tell you good-bye. Do you like your accommodations? I've been keeping this little getaway for years and when you messed up my plans, I just knew this was going to be the perfect place to take you. I can't have them finding you for some time. I need to collect my money and get out of the States before that happens. And by the time they find Jason and his lovely companion what's her name, you'll be a frozen stiff. That is if the animals don't decide to snack on you first."

They were in a rundown building, a house, she thought. The windows were busted out and there didn't seem to be anything in the place but some worn carpet and some tattered material that might have once been curtains at the window frames. She was tied to a chair by her arms and legs and there was a rag in her mouth. She wanted to scream at him, but he had taken that chance away.

"I can see by your face that you have questions. Well, I don't have time for them today. Why don't you put them in an email and send them to me?" His maniacal laughter bounced off the empty walls and through the house.

Her box of things and her purse were sitting by the chair. He had taken her coat off and her shoes and she could feel the cold seeping into her at an alarming rate. If she stayed here all night, she would be dead by morning. It was supposed to drop to below zero tonight. She knew this because she had been excited about the temperature change when she moved to Florida—an eighty degree change.

"I must be off now. You have a good life, well what's left of it anyway. I shall think of you often when I'm spending my millions." He leaned over and kissed her on the cheek and hugged her to him. Screaming behind the gag, she watched as he waved and moved out the door. A few minutes later, she heard the car start and then it too was silent.

She was going to die. Right here in this cold room tied to a chair. Twisting her arm around as best she could, she could see that it was just after three in the afternoon. She knew it was afternoon because even though it was cloudy, the sun was still out. Her feet were beginning to burn and her nose was running. She wondered fleetingly if she'd be covered in snot when they pulled her frozen body out, if they ever found her.

Taylor didn't hold out much hope that Cait would be able to find her. She didn't even know where she was. Moving her fingers, she felt the burn on the tips, the cold making them hurt when she tried to grip them. She didn't want to die. She wanted to go somewhere warm and bask in the sun.

The only thing that kept her going was the knowledge that the Feds would be all over this and Paul wouldn't be able to touch a penny of that money. She tried to imagine him going to the bank with his crisp suit and nice warm winter coat and a withdrawal slip. She wondered if he would come back and get her for it and giggled. Taylor remembered that agent telling her that even if he tried to take out one dollar, they'd be right there to get him. That gave her comfort.

Noises started to make their way into her consciousness. First, she thought she heard a wolf howling. Then as it got darker and colder, she heard music. It was getting harder and harder for her to stay awake and her feet no longer burned. She couldn't feel them or her hands. She knew they were there; she could see them, but they looked funny. She couldn't figure out what it was, but they just did.

When she opened her eyes again, she could see something in the room with her. It was looking in her box. She thought she had a couple of candy bars in there and wondered if the rat who pulled them out would share with her. She could go for a nice bit of chocolate and she loved frozen candy bars. She didn't know how they were going to get past the gag, but she figured if she asked really nice, he'd chew through it for her. But no biting me, she thought. Nope, won't do to bite the hand that feeds you. She giggled again.

The room was black as pitch when she came awake again. She couldn't move, but she thought she could hear the whop-whop of a chopper. Then a tune popped into her head and she started humming it. She thought it was the song from one of those police shows. But she wasn't sure. And Ratty was gone. He hadn't shared his dinner. Nor had he nibbled her gag off. Damned ungrateful rat. She'd have to have a talk with his mother.

Margaret was so nice. Taylor was sure she'd share her meal with her—and her covers. She wondered if Ratty had any brothers and if they hated her too. I'm not overly likeable, she thought to her friend the rat.

Drifting in again, she could see lights and wondered if the rat had invited his friends for dinner. There were only two bars in the box; surely he didn't think there was enough to feed that many. And they had no drinks to offer them. Maybe they'd lie down on her feet, if she still had them. It had been a long time since she'd had any feelings down there.

Voices woke her the next time. One of them kept telling her to wake up. Her rats were very smart and she was proud of Ratty for teaching them to talk, but they were too noisy. Then she felt warmth. The rats, they'd covered her up.

"So nice, Ratty. I love you." She drifted away again, thinking she was going to have frozen rat bodies attached to her when they found her.

Chapter Twenty-Two

Byron was pacing the living room when the phone rang. He had long since given up on trying to find out any information from the Feds who were climbing out of the wall at his mother's house. Cait had been really good about relaying what she could, but they still hadn't found Taylor. It was nearly two in the morning and the temperature was sixteen below out.

"They found her. She's alive, but she's nearly frozen. He had tied her to a chair in an open house and took most of her clothes off. They're taking her to OSU now by life flight. She'll be there in thirty minutes. She's...she's in good shape and their trying to warm her up. Her core temperature is eighty-three, they're worried about her kidneys and lungs, but they think they've found her in time. One of my men will take you to her and the rest of us will follow. Byron, she'll need support when she lands. The medics said she was hallucinating when they found her."

Byron grabbed Cait and kissed her. He wanted to be there when they landed and she knew this. Grabbing his coat, he was nearly to the car when he rushed back in the house.

"Jamie, you coming? We have to hurry." Then he went out again.

"She won't let them sedate her. She's been screaming since they took off. And she punched a medic in the nose. Damn, that girl is a fighter. If they can't get her under control soon they're going to have to tie her down." Damon was telling them this as they watched the helicopter make it's descent on the hospital pad.

"Let Byr go to her. He'll get her to calm down. She'll listen to him." Byron looked at Jamie. Neither man said a word and after a few seconds, Damon nodded and walked away.

"Are you going to be all right with me doing this to her? She's going to need me to be firm, very firm with her to cut through the pain." Byron didn't want to hurt her, but if she didn't let them help her, Damon said she could lose toes.

"Yes. If anyone can do this, you can. I love her too, Byr. I can't let her suffer because I'm a little creeped out by what she needs sexually. I guess what you both need. Just get her better. I need to have a long talk with her."

As soon as the helicopter landed, Byron was ushered to it. It was bitter cold with the wind blowing and he was grateful to be inside once the doors were closed over them. Then he heard her screaming.

"Ratty, help me! Daisies, daises! I hurt, I hurt so bad, please make it stop. I won't tell anyone, let me go back to him. Daisies! I love him and I didn't tell him. I fucking hurt!"

It would have been funny if it weren't so severe. The two medics in the main area were well away from her, as far as they could be in the tight confines of the workstation. The guy sitting the furthest away was covered in blood and his nose was swelling. Byron knew just how he felt.

"She has a hell of a left hook, doesn't she? I was told I could try to get her to calm down. They cleared it with the doctor inside. It's a little...different."

"I told them she was using her safe word and they told me I was nuts. Is she yours?" Byron looked at the pilot and nodded. "Thought so. She'll need a firm hand. I couldn't help and these two wanted to tie her down. Help the girl; she's been through enough, I think."

Byron went to the back and the one with the broken nose went to the front to sit and wait. She was sobbing now and fighting at the one restraint they had managed to get on her. Byron wanted to gather her in his arms and hold her, but as much pain as she was in, he knew she'd hurt him too.

"Slave! Slave! Listen to me!" He heard the hiss of the man in the front, but chose to ignore him. Bryon heard the pilot say something, but he was too busy to care. "Slave! You'll stop this right this minute!" Taylor immediately stopped fighting, but the tears were coming faster now.

"I hurt. Please, master. I hurt. Daisies. I said it, now make it stop. Please make it stop. I hurt so bad."

"I know, baby, but you have to let them treat you. I can't help you until they get you some pain meds. Tell me where you hurt." Damon said it was important that they knew the extent of her injuries and if she could feel her feet and fingers.

"My whole body. I think the rats saved my feet, but he wouldn't share the chocolate with me. I tried to make him do it with my mind, but he was...Byron, I hurt. Make it stop. I burn everywhere." Her sobbing broke his heart and he gathered her in his arms. She tried to wrap her hands around him, but the restraint stopped her. In a second, she was screaming again.

It took him longer this time to get through to her. But with him holding her, they were able to sedate her. After another ten minutes, she was quiet again. A few minutes more and she was out. They moved her into the hospital and straight to Intensive Care.

By noon, Taylor was sleeping quietly and the Grant household — all of them, including Margaret — were camped out in her room with her. Byron had crawled into the bed with her as soon as Damon approved. She still had slight tremors and Damon thought having Byron close would stop those altogether. By Christmas night, they knew she was going to be fine.

"You guys should go home and rest. I'll call if anything changes. I just want to hold her for a little while longer."

Byron wanted to take her home and put her in his bed, but he knew right now she needed what they were doing for her. Plus, there was a Federal Agent outside her door. They hadn't been able to locate Paul Freedom yet and that worried everyone.

~~~

Taylor opened her eyes and looked in front of her. She couldn't see much, the room was dark, but she could just make out shapes. Someone was lounging in a chair and she could hear them snoring. A light was coming from under a door and there were noises that sounded like sticky paper being walked on. Moving slightly, she

177

felt something tighten around her waist and she started to pull away when someone spoke.

"Shhhh, it's all right, I have you. Rest. I have you." Byron. He was spooned up behind her and holding her. His voice was slightly slurred and it was the greatest thing she'd ever heard in her life.

Turning slowly, she lay on her back and looked at him. His eyes were closed, but she was sure he wasn't sleeping; if he was, it wasn't very deep. She wanted to touch him, but didn't want to disturb him any more than she already had.

Her body hurt, but not like it did before. Her mouth was sore and when she reached up to touch it, she noticed her hands were raw and red. Touching her lips, she moaned at the pain she felt there as well.

"It'll heal. Damon said you were lucky. Your lips are chapped and you have a cold sore on your lower lip. But you have all your fingers and your toes." His whispered comment startled her.

Taylor looked at Byron and tears blurred him for a second. "I don't feel very lucky right now. He wanted to leave me there so that I'd freeze to death. How did you find me?"

"The phone. Even with the battery dead, the FBI was able to trace it because of the GPS chip in it. How do you feel, baby?"

"I don't...scared, cold, warm, terrified, stupid...I'm pretty sure the list is endless. Are you okay? You look so tired."

"I am tired. And you aren't stupid. You were kidnapped by a madman and rescued. Cait said that if you hadn't picked up the phone, we probably...she was impressed with your calmness too."

She looked at him for a few more minutes, her mind and body too tired to do much more than that. When Byron pulled her close to him, she felt warm, safe and loved. Closing her eyes felt good and within a minute, she was asleep again.

The next time she woke, the room was alight with sunshine. She moved slowly and with care because she was still sore. Her wrists were bandaged and moving her feet, she could feel the bandages on her ankles as well. She remembered being tied to a chair and wondered if that was what had happened. Snatches of things flittered through her mind, but nothing she could grasp.

The room she was in was nice, much like the first one she had woke in at Thanksgiving. There was a nice sofa and two large, overstuffed chairs. An area rug was in the center of the room and a large screened television took up most of the area above a bank of doors. There was a set of floor to ceiling windows on the wall to her right and though the curtains were closed, she could see it was a sunny day. She shivered thinking about the cold and pulled the blanket up over her more. Flowers were on nearly every available surface and a huge fruit basket was sitting on the end of a small table. She was just closing her eyes again when the door opened.

A woman in a crisp white uniform walked in with a man in a suit behind her. He nodded once to Taylor and then looked around the room, the bathroom, and even opened the closets, but he didn't say anything.

"Hello, Ms. Bennett. How are you feeling this morning? I'm Shanna, your nurse for this shift. I've come to take your blood pressure. This is Federal Agent O'Neill; he's the quiet type. Oh, and I'm to tell you Mr. Grant will be in to see in around nine."

"What time is it now? And how long have I been here?" Taylor was sure a few days had passed, but not sure how many.

"It's Tuesday, and just after seven-thirty. You've been here since Christmas morning, about three days now."

When Shanna was wrapping up her equipment to take out, she turned back to Taylor. "Can I get you anything? I don't think you're on solid foods yet, but I can get you something to drink."

"Do you think I could have some hot tea? And maybe another blanket, please? I'm cold." Taylor was sure it was just her mind and not her body that was cold, but she didn't care.

Ten minutes later, Taylor was drinking perhaps the worst cup of tea she'd ever drank and loving it. It was too sugary sweet and much too hot, but it was warming her on the inside and the sugar felt good on her belly. The blanket Shanna had brought in was warmed and she was soon asleep. Damon Grant woke her at eight-fifteen. Agent O'Neill was right behind him, performing the same search of the room. He stood by the door again while Damon approached the bed.

"Hello, sweetheart. How are you feeling today?" He checked her eyes and her ears for her and when he had her open her mouth, she felt like a horse for sale. She didn't say anything. She wasn't sure of this Grant.

179

"Cold. When can I go home? I know I've missed my plane, but I'm sure I can cash it in under the circumstances, don't you?" If she hadn't been looking at him, she might have missed the look he glanced her way. "What is it? What aren't you telling me? I have a right to know."

"I don't know what you mean. As far as you going home, it might be a few more days. I want to make sure the rawness in your hands and feet clears a little more. The cold sore on your lip is healing already and you don't seem to be having any ill effects from the extreme cold. If you think you can hold it down, I can order you some more solid foods and if that doesn't bother you, I'll switch you to regular foods tomorrow. I would like for you to try and get up. If you think you can, I'll have the nurse come and take the catheter out."

"Yes, please. On everything, food and the catheter. And I want to know what you're not telling me. I'm not stupid. That guy has been in here twice already looking in the doors like he's expecting Jack the Ripper to jump out and kill me. Tell me." The energy she had when she woke was draining away and she was ready to go back to sleep, but he wasn't going to put her off.

"Taylor, you're fine. Donald is here for your protection and he is —"

"He'd better be here for yours if you don't fucking tell me what's going on. Now spill it or I'm calling your mother! I know she'll make sure I know."

"Damn it, why is it that whenever there's news to be...Paul Freedom is still out there. The Feds, oh, pardon me, the FBI is afraid he'll come back and finish the job. He tried to access the money, but of course couldn't. He may be under the assumption that you have it."

"Why would he think...the account. He thinks because my name was on the account that I took it from him. And I don't suppose the newspaper had explained that the Feds have the money and not me." The agent had the good sense to look away. "I see. They're using me as bait. And when he comes here to 'finish the job,' am I supposed to just let him waltz in and shoot me or does someone have a plan?"

"The plan is to keep you safe and we will. Hello, sweetie. How are you feeling today?" Devin. The reason she was in this shit.

"Just peachy. You know, you're the reason lawyers have a bad reputation. I came to you in good faith and you feed me to the wolves. I want to go home. I don't care how you do it. I want to go home."

She burst into tears and pulled the blanket up over her head and sobbed. She didn't care if they stayed or not. She was having a hissy fit and they could damn well deal with it. She must have dozed off again.

When she opened her eyes this time, she wasn't alone in the room. Cait and Morgan were sitting in the chairs and Ronnie was on the couch holding her baby.

"Was it the tears or the fit that had them calling you guys in? And where's Agent Fed? He scared too?" Ronnie laughed and Morgan grinned. Cait just sat back and looked at Taylor.

"Both, I think. I know that Devin hates tears. Damon is pissed that he couldn't tell you anything and refused to come back until we let him explain. Don't you care where Bryon is?"

Yes, she did. Every time she woke up, she wanted to ask, but didn't know how. He would be there if he wanted to be and apparently, he didn't.

"I'm not his keeper and he's not mine. I'm sure he has plenty to do that doesn't involve me or my little problems." Taylor looked over at Ronnie when she snorted.

"Sure. I believe that like I'm going to not have a fight with Devin today. Byron is so head over heels in love with you it's scary. He's at home setting up a security system. The guys needed him there to make sure they did just what he wanted. He was supposed to be here by this afternoon, but they ran into a problem with the townhouse."

Security system? "Did someone threaten him? What does he need security for? I've been to his house; it's like Fort Knox now." All three women laughed. Taylor wished they'd let her in on it or go home.

"It's for you, you dork. He's having the system put in so you'll feel safe at his home. I think he's even having one put in the studio."

"I'm not staying at his house! I'm going home as soon as doctor stick in the mud lets me. I think the airline is going to let me reuse my ticket under the circumstances and I'm out of here."

The agents from Devin's office came in just as she was telling the women she was leaving. Agent Fenton looked like he'd just eaten lemons. She wondered if the man knew how to smile.

"We can't allow you to leave, Ms. Bennett. There are quite a few things we need to clear up first. And there is a killer on the loose who could be coming back —"

"Yeah, yeah, I've heard, come back to finish the job. I played my part and you know he's guilty. I'm done with you people. I don't know how much more I can be helpful. I don't know where he is. I don't even care anymore. I'm not a human popsicle and I have all my toes and fingers. If you need to complete some sort of test to file with your paperwork then by all means, ask your questions. I'm really tired and I just don't have the energy to deal with this anymore."

Chapter Twenty-Three

By the time they left, Taylor was barely hanging on. She was exhausted and her head hurt. The only good thing out of it was that the insurance companies had decided to give her a finders-fee of one percent of the money she found. Thirty-two hundred dollars would go a long way to setting her up in a nice apartment and maybe enough left over for a car. She was sound asleep when she felt the bed shift and startled awake to find Byron getting into bed with her.

"What do you think you're doing? You've been gone all day and now you come here thinking to sleep. I don't think so, buddy. I've had a shitty day and you are so not going to get to cuddle with me."

"I've missed you. And if you let me lay down with you, I promise to give you a treat—a nice one too." He held up a bag of her favorite chocolate candy bars, the tiny snack kind too.

"I can't have them yet. Damon said I needed to be able to hold down my dinner and they haven't brought it yet. Can I keep them for later? I'll let you play with my nipples if you say yes."

He laughed at her and pressed her back against the bed. "If you let me suckle at your nipples, I'll tell Damon you already ate and you didn't have a bit of problems with it." She groaned when he cupped her breast and when he rubbed his thumb over her hard peak. She arched up into his hand.

His hot mouth covered her nipple and he nipped at it none too gently through the material of her gown. Stars danced behind her eyelids and she wanted to strip him down and ride him.

"Please, Byron. I need you to touch me. Heat me, please? I need you so much." She heard the snaps release at the arms of the gown and suddenly his tongue was lapping at her nipple, nipping at the peak and worrying it with his ring. When he settled between her legs, she wrapped her ankles around him and was so glad that they had removed the catheter earlier that day.

"I know you're tender, baby, and I'll try to be gentle, but I need to be inside of you. I need to feel you around me. Please, tell me it's all right. Tell me you want this too."

"Yes. Hurry, please. I'm so wet and needy, I won't last long."

When he sat up on his knees between her legs and began working at his pants button, she slapped his hand away and pulled the tab down herself. Reaching into his pants, she was surprised to meet flesh and not his boxers. Wrapping her hand around him, his hiss made her realize he was just as needy as she was. When she leaned forward to take him in her mouth, he stopped her with his hand in her hair.

"No, no time. I want to be inside of you now. I need to feel you wrapped around me." Lifting her gown up, bare beneath, he reached between her spread legs and slid his fingers into her pussy. "Wet. Wet and hot. I thought I could be gentle, but not now. I'm sorry, baby, but I don't think I can hold back."

"Shut up and fuck me. Please, Byron, just come inside of me and stop talking about it." His chuckle made her groan and when he leaned forward, he entered her in one long, slick movement.

He filled her. The walls of her sheath grabbed him and she could feel it adjusting to his size. The pain was so slight that it was gone before she could complain, not that she would. Then he started to move, slowly as if he had all the time in the world. Her body wanted more and she reached down and grabbed his ass and pulled him into her while she tilted her hips. He was deeper; she could feel his balls touch her ass and when he pulled out to the tip and slammed back in, she nearly cried out with it. Everything, all of her, was focused on him and what he was doing to her. When he pulled her nipple into his mouth again and bit her, she came apart. She was sure if he hadn't put his hand over her mouth gently, she would have had a lot of explaining to do. But when he roared into her, and she came again, she couldn't stop the small scream that spilled from her mouth.

Immediately, the pounding at the door had them scrambling to right their clothes and the blankets. She knew that the door was locked when the agent on the other side yelled he was going to shoot the lock off is someone didn't "fucking answer him right fucking now."

Byron pulled his pants together and went to the door. Taylor had to put a pillow over her mouth to keep from being heard when Byron tried to hide his just laid look from the guard.

"We're okay. I just...I startled her when I got in bed with her. My...umm, my hands were cold. You know how women are when you touch them with cold hands. They get all jumpy. We're all right, agent, I swear."

When the door shut and the lock was turned again, Taylor couldn't stop the laughter. Her body ached with trying to hold it in and more so when she had let it out. Byron stalked back to the bed and removed his shirt before sliding in beside her.

"You know the least you could have done was quit laughing. I'm sure he was wondering what the hell was so funny. He looked ready to shoot me, I'll have you know."

"Cold hands, indeed. You have the warmest hands I've ever felt. Besides, I'm pretty sure he knew what we were doing anyway. You're very noisy when you come, did you know that? I've never known anyone who roared like a lion when they came. Now, you've worn me out and I'm very tired." She turned to her side and pulled away from him. In seconds, she was pulled back to his chest and wrapped in his arms. Warmth spread through her quicker than the warmed blanket had earlier.

She woke to feel him leaving the bed. When she turned to see him, he was getting dressed again. She wanted to ask where he was going and realized it was none of her business. And if he wanted to only have sex with her then she was fine with that. Or at least she'd try to be. When he kissed her good-bye with a quick, "I'll be back later," she barely made it until he shut the door again before she started crying.

When she woke up later in the morning, Jamie was sitting in the chair. His smile went a long way to making her feel better. And the real breakfast he'd brought her did so much more.

"You can eat it. I picked it up when Damon said you could have real food. Byron had me order it for you. He said to tell you he'd see you at noon and he'd bring you lunch. How you feeling?"

"Fine. I'm going home soon, I hope." She told him about the insurance money and how excited she was about being warm again. He gave her the same odd look Damon had given her the day before. Shrugging it off as a brother thing, she ate with gusto.

"I wanted to talk to you about when you were hurt before. I was—"

"Don't, Jamie. Forget it. We're friends and friends fight." He leaned forward and took her hands in his. His kiss on the bruises on her wrist made her wince, not from pain but because he noticed them and knew where they had come from.

"I'm glad we're friends, Taylor. I'm sorry about the way I treated you. I was an ass. I have—no let me finish. I have felt horrible about it for weeks and I wanted to thank you for sticking to it and not writing me off."

"I couldn't write you off, Jamie. You're like a really expensive bra to me. And I know expensive bras."

"You wanna explain to me how I compare to a bra? I'm glad it's an expensive one, but a bra, Taylor?"

"Sure, you're supportive when I need you to be. You lift me up when I'm down and I don't want to throw you away at the end of the day because you pinched me in all the tender areas. See? An expensive bra does that and more."

He laughed so hard he had tears streaming down his face and had one of the nurses come in to see what was so funny. When he told her, she looked at him with such a serious expression and said, "Well that's a hell of a compliment." He started laughing again. He went to the bathroom to blow his nose and cool off his face. The door opened again and this time, it wasn't a nurse.

This time, when the door opened, it was Paul Freedom. And he was pissed beyond words and he had a gun. A gun that was pointed at her.

~~~

186

Byron saw the cruisers as soon as he pulled into the lot. Nine of them lined the front of the hospital and all the doors were still open. His heart started pounding even before he was told the elevator was down and the hospital was on secure alert. Damon was paged and came down to meet him in the emergency room. A cop came instead.

"Taylor! Is she all right? What's happened? Is she all right?"

"I don't know, sir. I was told there was one dead and that the FBI guy had been drugged." They were on their way up the three flights of stairs when Byron had to stop and bend over to stop from passing out. Taylor, he'd not protected her.

They burst through the door of the stair well when Damon and Devin came rushing at him. He could tell by the look on their faces that something had happened. Captain Tucker was close behind them.

"Boy, I need you to put this in your pants. Put it in the back and agree with every word I say or hell will be paid. Understand me?" Captain Tucker was Cait's boss and he suddenly noticed that she was standing there too. She took the gun from him and slipped it in the waist band of his jeans. The cold metal made him shiver.

"Taylor, is she all right? Please, someone has to tell me what's happened." He was nearly sobbing now. Damon grabbed him, sat him in one of the chairs, and pushed Bryon's head between his knees as he spoke.

"They're both fine. The Feds won't let us in until they're done taking pictures, but they're both fine. If not, I'm going to rip that Agent Fenton's ass open with my hands."

"You'll have to stand in line," Cait mumbled. "Byron, Jamie killed Freedom. He came into the room demanding where his money was and he fired at Taylor. Jamie killed him. That's all we know for now."

"I don't understand, where did Jamie get a gun? I didn't think he even knew how to fire one." Byron sat up as he spoke. "You know, there are very strange things going on around here lately. I think I might need a vacation."

"Maybe a honeymoon? Jamie's been taking lessons at the college and I helped him qualify for his Concealed Handgun card. Here come the Feds." She stood in front of him and Byron laughed.

"Mr. Grant. That little girlfriend of yours, she's a spitfire, isn't she? I told her she needed protection. I just didn't know her protection would be coming from one of your brothers. You carrying?"

"Yes." Byron stood up, pulled out his wallet, and handed the agent his own card and drivers license. "I have a Glock on my ass and another on my ankle, both loaded both hot. There's also a card there that has my attorney's name on it. I own a club, Agent Fenton. I'd be stupid not to carry a gun. I want to see my 'little spitfire,' as you called her. Right now." They both turned to look at Cait when she burst out laughing.

"You think something's funny, Captain Grant?" Agent Fenton asked as he glared down at her. He didn't look amused.

Byron was surprised by the title, but didn't say anything. Stranger and stranger.

"No, not really. I was just thinking how the men in this family will surprise you at every turn and about the time you get them figured out, they fool you again."

Byron winked at her and then turned back to the Agent. "My fiancée, please?"

"She and your brother are being processed for crime scene evidence. I could charge your brother with carrying in a hospital zone, but if he hadn't have acted, then no telling how many would have died."

"Plus, it's a terrible blow to your department to know that a Federal Agent was low when a citizen took down the bad guy," Damon snarled at the agent. "A college professor at that. I'd really hate to put in my report that the officer in charge of guarding a witness in a huge insurance fraud scandal was being pampered by a pretty little nurse when shots were fired."

"Agent O'Neill was poisoned and you know it! You can't put lies in your report. Why...you will be falsifying government records." Agent Fenton flustered a bit and Byron grinned.

"You play right by mine and I'll play right by yours. Deal?" Cait's hand was out and the agent looked ready to break it rather than wanting to shake it, but Cait was never one to back down.

"Deal. But the next time I deal with this department, I want Captain Tucker to do it. You're too emotional. Plus, you have a damned family member at every turn."

No one said anything until the man was nearly to the elevators, then Cait sat down hard. Byron pushed her head between her legs and knelt in front of her.

"You bluffed, didn't you? Cait, what am I going to do with you? What if he'd have called?"

"He couldn't. I wasn't lying. I told him it would have been in my report, not the one I gave to him. Go see if they'll let you see Taylor. I'm sure Jamie could use you about now. They took the body out while we were talking to dick face."

Byron went to the door to her room and no one tried to stop him. Thank goodness, he wasn't sure he'd have been able to not hurt someone if they had.

When he opened the door, a nurse was helping Taylor from her bed. Blood covered her face and the entire front of her gown. The bed was also splattered with it. There was a pool of it on the floor and the area rug, which had been there this morning, had been removed too. Dizziness swamped him and suddenly, he was pulled into a hug and held onto his brother. Jamie had saved her. It took him a few seconds to realize he was whispering in his ear.

"It's not hers. It's his. He didn't hit her. I killed him. Byron, the blood isn't hers, I swear. I checked her myself. Are you listening to me? Byron, she's fine. They have to take her gown for evidence so you can't touch her. Just hold me. I need...I killed him. He'll never hurt her again. She's fine."

Byron tightened his grip on his brother and pulled him to his body, brother to brother. They were both crying. Neither said a word, but each knew that whatever else happened in their lives, this one defining moment made them closer than brothers would ever be. Byron walked to the bathroom door where Taylor had been taken and knocked.

"Just a minute. I need to help her in the shower. Then when she comes out you can—"

"You can open the door on your own or I bust it down. Your choice. I'd prefer that you let me kick it in, but like I said..."

He heard Taylor's laugh and then the click of the lock opening. She was sitting on the toilet with a gown draped over her front. She had a smile that melted his anger away.

"You couldn't have waited for five more minutes, could you?" The nurse bared the door from him. "Now you have to go back out so that she can get cleaned up. We've taken the pictures of her and now she wants a shower."

"I'll be giving her a shower. Then she'll be coming home with me. I suggest you have the proper paper work filled out and signed when we're done or Damon Grant will be pissed. Now, get out."

The nurse huffed for a minute, but Taylor and Byron barely noticed. They could only see each other. When the door slid closed behind them, Byron took the gown away from her and tossed it on the floor. And then he started to unbutton his shirt.

"We're going to take a shower to clean you up then I'm taking you back to my house. I don't want to hear a word about what happened here right now and I don't want to hear another word about you leaving me. Understand?"

"Byron, I don't—"

"Not a word. Then when we rest and I feed you, I'm going to make love to you all day. You'll not leave my bed for anyone or anything. And as soon as it can be arranged, I want you to marry me. I can't...Taylor, I love you with all my heart and I need you. Please, I need you." He took his pants off and held them in his hand and she still hadn't said a word. "Taylor?"

"Oh, now I can talk? Thank you so much. First of all, you pigheaded asswipe, I love you too. But I will not be ordered around and I will not just jump when you say do it. I'm a person. I have feelings and moods and I have a mind. A fucking good mind too. If you don't like it then you can just kiss my ass. I am going to tell the police what happened now. Not tomorrow when you've satisfied some sense of protectiveness, now! I want this over with. I want it finished. Then if you're really nice to me, I'll go home with you and I might just let you make love to me. But from here on out, we make decisions, not you alone. Do you understand?"

He just stared at her with a cocked brow. Damn, Byron thought. There wasn't any mood she didn't look beautiful in. He reached into his pocket and pulled out the box. Dropping to one knee, he sat in front of her and took her hand.

"I've been to seven different jewelers over the past two days. I wanted to find the perfect ring for you. Today, I helped take my mother home from the hospital and she reminded me that I had my great grandmother's ring still in the safe at home. I'd forgotten about it. When I saw it, I knew that I'd found the ring for you. If you don't like it, I can get you anything you want, but with this ring, I want to declare my love for you." He opened the box and when her face lit up, he knew that he'd made the right choice. "Taylor Mae Bennett, will you please be my wife? Will you be my playmate, my partner? Will you love me forever and keep me sane? Taylor, will you please put me out of my misery and marry me?"

"Byron, I don't know. What if you meet someone who really rocks your—" He simply cocked a brow at her again. "Okay, yes. I'll marry you. I love you."

"Thank God! We'll get married on Valentine's Day. That is, if you want to. I'd like for it to be sooner, but Mom said she was going to have a party and you were going to let her do it. I've already talked to Ben and he'll make...with your approval, he'd like to make a dress for you. This is going to be hard."

"I know, but I have faith in you. And I'll be more than glad to help you. By the way, I think you have a punishment coming."

He slid the ring onto her finger and kissed it. Her mouth was still swollen so he gave her the briefest kiss and both hungered for more. But she needed to get the blood off her and he wanted to hold her. He picked her up, pulled her to him, and turned on the shower.

Chapter Twenty-Four

"No. I told you this already eight times. I didn't know Jamie had a gun, but I'm damned glad he did. I didn't know that Paul was going to come in and try to kill me. Don't you think that is by far the stupidest question you've asked me — twelve flipping times now? Why the hell would I just be laying there if I knew he was going to come in and try to kill me? If this is the way you guys conduct an investigation, I'm glad I didn't depend on you to save me. He came in the door demanding that I tell him where his money was and then he started waving the gun around. Jamie had gone to the bathroom to blow his nose, just as I told you the first time you asked me. He came out and when Paul fired at me, Jamie fired back. I didn't see Jamie's gun. I was too focused on the one that was currently being pointed at my head. I didn't see if Jamie had it out when he came out of the bathroom; again, the gun pointed at my head had my full attention. When Jamie fired his gun, Paul sort of exploded. The left side of his head just went...it went everywhere, including on me. Do you have any idea what it feels like to have someone's brains splattered all over your body? Not a thing I'd like repeated. I think I've told you this story enough. I'm tired and I want to go home and have sex with Byron. If that's too blunt for you, then fuck off."

Damon burst out laughing then tried to cover it with a cough. Devin looked at her wide-eyed for about ten seconds and then he, too, started laughing. She could feel Byron laughing behind her and his hands squeezed her arms in approval.

Taylor had tried to be nice, but they'd been at it for over three hours. She had to smile when she thought of the look on Agent Fenton's face when he asked who was staying for the interview.

"I'm her lawyer and she isn't saying a word without me. Damon is her doctor. If you tire his patient, he'll kick your ass. So both of us." He turned to Byron.

"And you are?" Fenton had stood up over her and Byron as they lay out on the fresh bed in a different room.

"Staying." And he had. He hadn't said a word either. He'd been holding her hand and sometimes rubbing her arms, but he never said a word to the agent.

"Ms. Bennett, the sooner we get this over with, the sooner I can let you go. If you'll just answer the question the way I want, it'll be finished. I want this solved as soon as possible too."

"Did you just threaten my client, Agent Fenton?" Devin moved to stand beside her as he asked. "Are you telling her that if she doesn't answer the questions the way you want them answered then she is in custody? That's what I heard. I think this meeting is over. The insurance company is happy and so am I. You're superior is also happy. I frankly don't give a shit if you are or not. Now. If you have any more questions for either Ms. Bennett or Mr. Grant you'll need to contact my office. Gentlemen."

Taylor went to the bathroom and put on the clothes that someone had brought her. There were some jeans, two shirts, a worn sweatshirt and two pair of socks. Her worn tennis shoes were there. There was also a thick, heavy coat and mittens. There was a beautiful box sitting on the counter and she opened it too.

A pair of the tiniest black panties she'd ever seen was nestled in the tissue paper and a little bra that had underwire and no cups. It, too, was black. Smiling and knowing who purchased them, she slipped them on. She had seen this set in the store the last time she'd been there and couldn't afford them. She couldn't wait to show them to Byron. She also put everything else on, including two pair of socks. They were making their way down to the exit when Byron's phone rang.

"Hello, Mom. I'm just taking Taylor home...yes, to my home. No, I didn't tell her. She made me ask her and she hasn't answered me yet...I don't know about that either. Hang on."

He handed her the phone and no matter how hard she tried to get away, he just overpowered her and she had to take it anyway.

"Hello, Mrs. Parker. How's your leg?"

"I think it's high time you started calling me Margaret. It's fine, dear. I was hoping I could convince you and Byr to come over for dinner. We've not had our Christmas yet and we wanted to celebrate."

"Why haven't you had Christmas yet? It's like the twenty-ninth or something, isn't it? I bet the kids are going nuts."

"We had to wait on you, dear. It wouldn't have been Christmas without all my family here, now would it? The children? Well, most of them are very small and Meggie is happy to have another aunt. By the way, I love that you're making him ask and not tell you, dear. He's very demanding. So what time should I expect you? Dinner is nearly finished, but we can eat it cold if you want us to wait."

Taylor muted the phone and looked at Byron. "I know where you get it from now. You are your mother's son. She wants us to come over and have Christmas. They actually held it for me to get better. Oh and if we make them wait, then we can eat it cold."

"I have the rest of my life with you, Taylor. I can wait one more day to have you. But this is going to cost you. You'll owe me a big punishment for this. I'll expect special allowances for allowing you this."

Taylor burned for him and she knew that he could see it in her eyes. She turned back to the phone and told Mrs. — Margaret that they'd be there in twenty minutes. Then she turned back to Byron. "You have a club close right?"

Dinner was a grand affair and when everyone was stuffed to the top, Taylor and Byron had been rushed in the house so quickly that there had been no opportunity to look around. She loved the house; the dining room was big and beautifully decorated for the holidays.

"We kept it decorated for Christmas. Usually, we're getting ready for the New Year's Eve bash we have. Some but not all the decorations are taken down and most of the furniture it put into storage. There are too many guests to allow for much else. You'll be here, of course. Maybe we can talk to Ben tonight and see what he can do for you as a dress."

"Mrs. Parker, I like to make my own decisions on my life. I know how to pick out a dress to wear. But I thank you very much."

"You might as well let her have her way in the dress department or you'll never hear the end of it. I think she's making up for not having a little girl to dress up when the boys were growing up." Dan sat next to her on the huge sofa.

Margaret was on the loveseat, her leg propped up on a few pillows. The woman still managed to look regal and suave. Taylor didn't feel uncomfortable around her and was surprised and pleased by that.

They discussed family and who to invite. Taylor had no one and looked over at Jamie and smiled. She thought of their friendship and hoped that they could once again be friends, if he'd ever forgive her. She got up and asked to speak to him in private. He didn't hesitate and that made her happy. They went to the large study.

"Byron asked me to marry him tonight and I said yes. I wanted to know, are you...because if you don't...I want you to be okay with it. I love you, Jamie, and I don't want to do anything to upset you."

She walked over to the large window in the room and looked out over the huge deck. It too had been decorated for Christmas. There was even a tree with gifts under it, brightly lit and very festive.

"I love you too, Ta. And I'm sorry. I was a jackass. I'm very happy for you. And I'm glad you're going to be my sister. It'll be official now. You and he suit, and I'm happy for you both."

"Good. Jamie, will you give me away? I don't have any family and you are the closest thing to a brother I've ever had. I would love for you to give me to your brother. Please?" She waited for what seemed an eternity and then looked back at him.

"You want me to give you away? Ah, Ta, I'd be honored to do that for you. The six of us usually perform the best men thing and we've been doing that a lot lately. Wait! I don't have to, like, pay for it or anything, do I? Sheesh, I heard Mom talking. I don't think I have enough for all she has planned for you guys."

"No, I'll pay my own way. I won't be able to afford the things she has planned either, but she'll get over it. I haven't a clue how much it'll cost, but I do have that insurance bonus coming. Maybe Byron and I can just go to the justice of the peace. He wants it to be soon anyway and I can probably afford that."

"Ta, I don't think my mother plans for you to pay for anything. I think she—"

"Oh, I've no doubt that's exactly what she thinks, but if she wants this to happen, then it happens my way. JP or we just live together for a while. It matters little to me. In fact, I'd rather we live together. Then if he finds someone else, we're fine and go our separate ways."

"Did you tell Byr this? I bet you didn't. I'm sure he'll have quite a bit to say about this, as a matter of fact. And my mother won't be happy if you live together either."

"Who's living together? Hello, love. Jamie, have you another woman living at your place? I will tell Mom this time." Byron came in, scooped her up in his arms, and settled her on his lap.

"Damn it, Byron, don't you knock? We were having a private conversation here. Go away. I'll come find you when we're—" Taylor started before Jamie cut her off.

"She's planning on paying for her wedding to you. And she thinks that living together might be better in the event you find someone else better than her in the meantime. She also thinks Mom is bossy."

"I didn't say that! But she is. James Grant! That was a low thing to do. Do you know the meaning of private conversation? I'm quite capable of taking care of myself."

"Jamie, do you think you can give us a few minutes. I'd like to have a conversation with my future wife. And lock the door on your way out. Tell Mom...tell her we may be a little while." She looked at him and could feel the coiled steel of anger coming off him.

Jamie winked at Taylor on his way by and then kissed her on the cheek. She wanted to punch him in the nose. He would pay for this, she'd make sure. The lock clicking into place when the door shut was loud in the silent room.

"You can't think to do whatever it is your thinking in your mother's house. She'll kill you then me. I want you to please wait until we get to your house."

"Up. And I want you to take off your clothes, now. And everything I have at this moment is yours as well. It's our house, our cars and our whatever else you will get when you marry me."

"I will not take off my clothes. I've just gotten warm. Besides, the children have waited long enough to open their gifts."

"Strip. Now, or so help me, I'll punish you so hard you'll beg me to stop. Right now you're just looking at a paddling. If you make me say it again, I'll think of something else to add to it." She felt her pussy gush with liquid heat and her nipples peak against the lace that barely covered them.

She looked at him and realized he was serious. Not about hurting her, he'd never do that, but he would make her suffer. She pulled the sweatshirt over her head along with the two undershirts. Unsnapping the jeans, she shimmied them off her slim hips and pulled them off with her two pair of socks and tennis shoes at the same time. She stood before him in the panties and bra set he had purchased her. When she reached up to take off the bra, he stopped her.

"Come here and assume the position. I want to feel how turned on you are. I need to feel how wet you are just thinking about me spanking your beautiful ass until it's red and heated."

Taylor stepped in front of him and spread her legs wide. Dropping her head low with her hands behind her back, she could see his hand reach forward and touch her mound. She knew she was soaking wet and knew that from where he was sitting, he could more than likely smell her. Another gush of cream flooded her panties when he pressed against her slit. When he slipped his finger under the silk and touched her clit, she couldn't help the moan of pleasure that spilled from her lips.

"You're so wet I could slide my cock into your pussy and never hurt you. Do you have any idea what that does to me, knowing that you're wet enough to drown me if I wanted to taste you? My cock aches to be inside of you, aches to feel you tighten around me and pull me into your depth."

198

When he leaned forward and moved the bit of lace aside, she felt her legs tremble with anticipation. Her breasts swelled and her nipples tightened into small stones. He didn't taste like she thought he would. He didn't even slide his fingers into her like she wanted to beg him to do. All he did was kiss the skin just above the lace and pull back. When he stood up and moved to the door, she wanted to scream at him.

"Get dressed and then come out into the living room. You aren't to touch yourself; you aren't to give yourself any relief at all. And I'll know if you do. I believe the children have waited long enough to get their gifts and I won't have your bad behavior ruin that for them." He was nearly to the door when he stopped and turned back to her. "Where are we going when we leave here tonight?"

It took her mind a few seconds to catch up to what he was saying. It was a trick and she almost didn't answer. "Our house."

"Good girl. And how will we get to our house?"

She wanted to say he was going by ambulance, but thought that would get her nowhere with him but into more trouble. "Our car." She could hear the anger in her voice and apparently, so had he. She was shaking with the need to hurl something at his arrogant head, but knew that he would make her pay if she did. Besides, she didn't think she would be able to explain how she came to be nearly naked when he was a dead body on the floor.

"You're going to pay for that. Hurry now, I think you've dallied long enough. And Taylor, when my mother asks, we are paying for our wedding. And whatever date she picks, you'll agree, understand me?"

"Yes. Byron?" His quirked brow is all she got in response. "Turnabout is fair play." She turned her back to him and pulled on her shirts. She was pulling on her jeans when she heard the door shut.

Chapter Twenty-Five

Bryon didn't go to the living room right away but went out on the deck. It was just about eight degrees out tonight and he thought maybe it would be just cold enough to take the edge off his need. Shutting the door behind him, he leaned against the railing and took several deep breaths.

Christ, she had him harder than a stone and he could swear he could ram a spike in a concrete wall with is cock. And he was fairly sure she knew it. Walking away just now was by far the hardest, stupidest thing he'd ever done. He was nearly ready to go back in there and finish what he'd started when the door opened behind him. He turned to see Nicky. He laughed when Byron groaned.

"It's not so bad really, having someone love you that much. Or you loving them. And it's definitely worth it. I wish I'd of been a lot smarter when I first met Morgan. But that's all behind us now. I know you love her. Taylor, I mean. You're different since she's come into your life."

"I do love her. And I feel different. We have a lot to work out. She's...she has an independent streak in her that irritates me to no end. And she makes me so mad sometimes all I want to do is beat her butt." Smiling, he thought that was the best part of Taylor. She loved to play as much as he did.

"I'm sure that poses no problem for you. I'd like to talk to you about her independent streak for a minute. I want to offer her a job. Well, Devin and I do. She did a fantastic job the afternoon she stayed at the office and with you working as well...maybe it'll give her a sense of self-worth."

"Self-worth, huh? And does everyone know about our lifestyle? Taylor told me that Mom asked her all sorts of questions about it. Oh well. Why are you asking me if she can work for you? She does make...Jamie. He told you I was mad about the wedding. We have that worked out. If she wants to work for you two, that's fine with me. I know she enjoyed herself. I know she'll be all right there." Neither man mentioned what had happened to Devin's secretary nearly a year ago.

Caroline had been killed when a madman had come and kidnapped Devin and tried to rape Ronnie. So much had changed since then and Byron knew that it would continue to change from now on. The two brothers talked for a few more minutes then went indoors. Taylor was sitting in one of the chairs from the dining room that had been brought in for the gathering.

The chair was sitting as far from the tree as possible and she was covered in a blanket with the fire from the fireplace at her back. He felt bad for making her strip when she'd said she was cold, but he was pretty sure she'd not felt it when she'd been standing there nearly naked in front of him. Heat surged through his body and he thought about going back out on the deck again.

"Come on, you two. We've been waiting. Whose turn is it to be Santa? I think it's your turn, Nicky. Get the hat and start passing them out." Even from her perch on the loveseat and her leg in a cast, Margaret Parker ruled like a queen.

Byron walked over to where Taylor was seated and watched as her eyes heated as she watched him. Need for this woman on so many levels rippled through his body. When he scooped her into his arms again and sat with her on his lap, she squeaked at him, glared then turned to ignore him. Pulling her back around, he kissed her soundly and then held her tight, purposely keeping his hand on the outside of the blanket.

Gifts were passed around and when Nicky handed one to Taylor, she turned to give it to Byron. She looked confused when Nicky said it was for her. She looked almost panicky.

"I thought this was for the children. I don't...I don't think...I don't want anything from you. I'm happy to just watch. It's okay." She let Byron pull her into his arms and he whispered in her ear.

"Honey, take the gift in the spirit it was given. My family is trying to say they want you to be a part of it. Now hush, say 'thank you, Santa,' and open it."

"Thank you, Santa," she whispered to Nicky, and then ruined it by bursting into tears. When she tried to pull away from him, he held her to his body and kissed her while she cried. Meggie came over and started talking to her. Before Byron could tell her what Meggie said, Taylor nodded, took the girl's hand, and they went to the bathroom. When they were out of the room, his mom asked what she said.

"Meggie told her she wanted to talk to her. I don't know about what. I wasn't sure Taylor could speak to her until this moment."

They continued to open gifts until the pair returned. After that, everything seemed all right. Meggie sat next to Taylor on the floor and they opened gifts together. Morgan winked at Byron and smiled.

Margaret had a hard and fast rule about unmarried couples sleeping together in a house of children. She didn't make any exception for any of her boys so Byron and Taylor packed up to go home. There were no fights. Byron not only loved his mother, he respected her and her home a great deal. But he needed Taylor much more than his need to wake up and have breakfast with his brothers. It took him over two hours to get to his house outside of Columbus. Sitting in the drive, he looked over at Taylor.

"Very few people have been here, including my family. You are the only woman that's ever been here and the last to spend the night with me. This isn't a home, but a house. It's decorated very nicely, but it's cold and too perfect. The house is yours, Taylor. Yours to do whatever you like, however you like. It's not a small house. There are eight bedrooms and nine bathrooms. A dining room big enough to seat fifty people and a kitchen to feed them all without resorting to outside help. I want you to hire help with it if you don't mind. I want you rested when I want you. I've never put in a play room, but I'd like to now, for us."

She looked at the house and then back at him. "You're brothers offered me a job. I think I'm going to take it. I can't wait for you to get up every day at the crack of noon. I'm a morning person. I don't know how to cook, but I think I'd like to learn. I know nothing about your business, but that, too, I'd like to learn." She sat for several seconds then looked at the house. "I've never owned anything before, just my car and my laptop. I've lived in crappy places forever, trying to make it work. I think I'd like to hire someone to help me learn how to do that too, learn how to run a house.

"Byron, are you sure about this? Are you sure you want to marry me? I don't have a thing to offer you but my love. I'd...I don't know anything about families. I don't know a thing about the closeness you have with yours. Are you very sure about this?"

"Yes. I've never been more sure about anything in my life. Knowing that for the rest of my life I'm going to have you in it makes me breathe easier. Knowing that you'll be by my side makes looking into our future seem more colorful. I love you, Taylor."

After they took all the gifts and Taylor's bags into the house, she was dragging. It was hard for him to remember that she'd been in the hospital just this morning and had witnessed the death of someone she knew. When she started slurring her words when she was moving up the stairs, he picked her up and knew when she didn't protest that she was beyond tired. She was asleep before he pulled her shoes off her.

~~~

Taylor woke to an empty bed. She wasn't sure where she was at first, but remembered that she had come home with Byron and he must have put her into the bed. All she had on was the black bra and panty set he'd bought for her. She went to his closet, pulled one of his shirts off the hanger, and was slipping it over her head when she left the bedroom. She found him in the study on the computer. He looked up when she stood in the doorway.

"I'm sorry I fell asleep. I guess I was more tired than I thought. What are you doing?" She walked toward him when he patted his lap.

"I'm looking at toys and trying to decide which ones we want. I was going to narrow down a list, then let you help me pick things out. Most of it is for your use and my benefit, but we can still pick together. Here, look what I've selected so far."

The screen showed a few pieces that she was familiar with and a couple she wasn't. When he clicked on one of the ones she didn't know, a demonstration for it came up, complete with couples using it. Her breath caught watching the people on the screen.

The "Hanger" was several chains hanging from the ceiling of the room with two leather straps on it. Within seconds, a nude man and woman walked in front of the camera and he started strapping her into it. She lay over the widest strap at her waist and had her ass hanging over the edge. The man took a small belt and buckled it over her lower back, holding her in place. When he reached between her legs and slid his fingers into her pussy, Taylor felt Byron's cock harden under her. When he slid his hand between her legs she opened for him, put her thighs over his, and leaned back.

"Watch what he does to her. I want to see you like this, naked and open for me. My friend from Paris sends me these to see what I think about them in my club. This one is going to be the first thing I get for us."

The man on the screen pulled out his fingers and licked them just as Byron slid his into her wet pussy. Taylor was breathing hard and having a hard time concentrating on the people on the screen when Byron started to fuck her with his hand.

Moving to the front of the woman on the screen, the man took the other strap and put it under her breasts. Then he buckled another belt over her back. Her arms where then brought up behind her and tightened behind her. A blindfold was put over her eyes and then the man walked off screen. Seconds later, the woman began to lift until she was no longer touching the floor. A slight swing to the chains made the woman look like she was hanging free, which Taylor supposed she was. The man entered again and this time, when he came up behind the woman, he put a stretcher between her ankles.

The stretcher was used to keep the person it was being used on to not be able to close her or his legs. It also opened up her pussy wide, and also her ass cheeks. On the video Byron and Taylor were watching, the woman's pussy was clean shaven and pink. The man's cock was long and hard. So was Byron.

When the man on the screen dropped to his knees and began eating the woman from behind, Taylor felt her own pussy cream and heat. And when Byron had her stand up and lean over his desk, she knew he was going to find her dripping, cream running down her thighs.

"He's enjoying that, tasting her. Would you like for me to show you how good it feels, Taylor?" He already had his fingers in her and moving in and out slowly.

"Yes. Please. Lick me like he is her. I want to feel your tongue deep inside of me." When she felt his breath on her thigh, she moaned. Knowing that he was going to do just what she wanted made her sway slightly.

"You need this, don't you, baby? You need to come so bad it's making you sweat. Well, I do too. I don't want you to hold back from me tonight. Whenever you feel the need to come, I want you to let it go. We've been too long restrained and I want to hear you scream for me."

The people on the screen forgotten, the couple that had been watching them so focused on each other there wasn't thing on earth that could keep them from making love tonight. When Taylor stood up and took off his shirt and her bra, she felt him tear her panties from her hips.

"It's going to be hard keeping you in sexy underwear if you continue to look this delicious in them. I promise to replace them if you let me rip them from you every night. I may have to invest in the company if we keep this up."

"Please, Byron. Less talk and more action. I need to feel you taste me. I love your tongue ring inside of me. I may get one just to pleasure you in the same way." His growl of approval was cut off when he buried his mouth in the line of her ass.

His tongue touched her tight ring and she opened her legs wider for him. No one had ever taken her there before and she was suddenly glad that Josh had told her it wasn't for him. Then Byron opened her cheeks with his fingers, slid one of his hands between her legs, and fingers into her pussy. Not another thought came into her mind.

With his fingers coated with her juices, he moved them up and began working them into her hole. Heat coursed through her and before she knew it, he had two fingers in her and he was scissoring them inside of her as he fucked her pussy with his free hand. The burning gave way to the most incredible pleasure she'd ever had.

"I'm going to fuck you here tonight. I need to make you mine and I want to feel this tight hole wrapped around me. I've been thinking about it for days. Are you all right with that?"

"Yes. I know it'll hurt, but I trust you. It feels so good to have you moving inside of me. I can't wait to feel your cock in me."

He stood up then and she heard the chair they'd been sitting in move away. He continued to work her ass hard and she felt the first stirrings of a climax moving through her. A drawer opening distracted her for a second then Byron was leaning over her. She could feel his cock through his jeans as he rubbed her ass with it.

"I have some lotion here I'm going to lube you with. Then I'm going to take off my clothes. Touch your pussy for me. Play with your clit while I get you ready. Come, baby. It'll make you looser when I enter you."

When he pulled his finger out of her, she moaned at the loss, but she slid her fingers into her dripping pussy and rode them hard as she heard him strip. Her heart was pounding by the time he touched her again and when he rubbed his cock up her seam of her ass, she tried to take him into her.

"Not yet. Christ, but you're soaking me. My cock is covered in your juices. I'm going to work you a bit more, but I honestly don't know how long I can wait. Your heat is scorching me back here and I want to feel you."

The cool lotion made her pull away slightly, but it soon heated too. When he slid his finger back into her, she looked down at the computer screen just as the man pulled out of the woman's pussy and started shooting his cum all over her ass. Taylor came with him.

Wave after incredible wave rushed over her and when Byron pulled out this time, she felt his cock nudge at her opening. Not even waiting to be told, she took a deep breath, leaned forward, and when she felt him push beyond her tight rings, she exhaled and relaxed her muscles. Byron pushed hard and with a pop, was deep into her ass.

Neither of them moved. Taylor hurt, burned from the inside out. She wanted to scream at him to pull out, but also wanted to please him more than anything in the world. When he leaned forward and kissed her shoulder, his movement brought on a sensation she didn't expect. A spike of pleasure so deep, she moved back against him to feel it again.

"Baby, I'm barely hanging on here. If you keep that up, I'm going to fuck you. If you behave, I might be able to pull out wit...holy Christ, don't...Taylor!"

Pleasure built on pleasure. His voice, strained hard from trying to hold back, had her wanting him even more. When he moved into her, with each stroke she moved back, riding the waves of overwhelming need for him to come in her. When he grabbed her hips and began pumping into her none too gently, she slid her fingers between her legs and began stoking her clit with one hand and fucking her with the other. With her face laying on the desk, her legs wide and open, she felt his balls slap hard against her pussy and she stretched her thumb out far enough to let his balls bounce of it every time he slammed into her.

"I'm coming, baby. Now, come with me. Christ!" She felt the first wave of his hot cum fill her and that set her off again. She screamed out his name as she came. The harder he pumped into her, the harder her pussy and ass clenched around him. Just when she thought she was finished, she came again.

When Byron collapsed against her back, his hot breath curling over her neck and shoulder, she smiled. He was as limp as she was, just as drained. When he kissed her shoulder, she shuddered, not from the cold but from the crushing need to take him into her arms and hold him to her. Giving into that need, as soon as he pulled his cock from her body, she turned and wrapped herself around him.

"I love you. I think I've love you since you came storming into my bedroom. Please don't leave me."

"Never. I love you too much. However, if we continue to have sex like this daily, I don't think I'll last as long as I'd like. That was the unimaginably wonderful. I never thought of myself as an ass man, but your beautiful little hole has made me a changed man. Please tell me you enjoyed that and that I didn't hurt you. We should have prepared you more, but seeing you like that, bent over and wet, it was all I could do not to slam into you right off."

"Yes, it was wonderful, better than I thought it would ever be. I'm so glad you've been my first. But now, I'm hungry and tired. I don't have to start working for your brothers until the New Year so we can sleep in tomorrow. I think I'll enjoy it too."

After a quick snack of cereal and milk, they both went to bed. This time, Byron stayed with her the entire night. At noon, when they woke to a ringing door bell, it was all Taylor could do to keep standing upright she was laughing so hard when Byron went stomping from the room. He really wasn't a morning person. When he came stomping back a few minutes later, saying the door was for her, she laughed harder when he crawled back into the bed and pulled the covers over his head.

Going to the front door, she was surprised to see a man standing in the foyer. He looked very nervous. In fact, he was shaking.

"That man coming back? He said if I had bad news or if I hurt you, he'd hunt me down. I don't think he was kidding."

"He's not a morning person. He said you had something for me? I don't know who would even know I was here except for his family."

The man handed her an envelope and had her sign. He was gone before she opened it up. There was another envelope inside and a sheet of paper.

"Taylor,

This came to our office today and the delivery person knows to bring them to our house until you start working for me. I thought this would make your new year.

The insurance company wrote you a check and had it couriered over this morning. Enjoy and have fun with it. But not too much. I'll help you with investments when you're ready.

Your favorite brother-in-law,

Devin"

She was halfway to the kitchen when she screamed and before she could sit down, Byron came into the room stark naked, brandishing a gun. She didn't know whether to scream again or laugh. She decided on the latter. Then she showed him the check.

The insurance company had paid off. They paid her one percent of the found fraudulent funds she'd found for them—all seven hundred and twenty-five million of it. Her cut was seven million two hundred and fifty thousand dollars.

"Byron, what am I going to do with all this? It's so much more than I thought it'd be. I'm rich!"

"You can buy breakfast. Later. Right now, I'm taking my very wealthy future wife back to bed." Picking her up and with a quick swat to her ass, off they went.

Byron

About the Author

I woke up one morning and decided to give play time to the people in my head who were keeping me awake. Little did I know that they would be so relentless and want their time right now! I wrote for the pure joy of it and to entertain my family and friends. But mostly it was to get more than an hour of sleep without a story playing out. Of course, the more I write, the more they want. So…well, as a result of sleepless days (I work through the night as a gun toting grandma – nope not a vigilantly but an armed security guard) I have lots of stories written.

Hello! My name is Kathi Barton and I'm an author. I have been married to my very best friend Sonny for at times seems several lifetimes – in a good way, honey. And together we have three wonderful children and then the ones we brought into the world - Paul and Dale Barton, Jason and Wendy Barton and Danielle and Ben Conklin. They have given us seven of the greatest treasures on Earth. They don't live at home seven days a week! No, seriously, seven grandchildren – Gavin, Spring, Ben, Trinity, Sarah, Kelly and Kian.

The Grant Brothers Series

Now Available

Coming Soon

www.ingramcontent.com/pod-product-compliance
Lightning Source LLC
Chambersburg PA
CBHW020618180626
46810CB00007B/2826